HIDDEN SECRETS

BLACKMOORE SISTERS COZY MYSTERY SERIES
BOOK 9

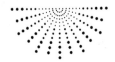

LEIGHANN DOBBS

SUMMARY

Morgan Blackmoore has a secret, and she's desperate to hide it from her sisters. So when local paranormal healer Clementine Vega is murdered and Morgan is accused of the crime, she has to do something she's never done before—lie to her family. But soon one lie turns into another, and she finds herself navigating a tangled web of deceit.

Now, with her sisters on the verge of war with paranormals, Morgan must uncover the killer's mysterious motive before her sisters spark a paranormal war that they might not win, or worse, before they discover the shocking secret that Morgan has been hiding from them.

CHAPTER ONE

*M*organ Blackmoore had a secret, and she was terrified that her sisters might discover what it was. For the first time in her life, Morgan felt isolated, her dark thoughts eating away at her and driving her to retreat from the people who were closest to her.

As she looked out the window of the old family cottage that she and her sister Fiona now used as their shop, Sticks and Stones, her thoughts were bleak like the early winter that had descended upon their seaside town of Noquitt, Maine.

Normally being here at the cottage made Morgan happy but not today. Set off the beaten path, the cottage was nestled in a forest filled with old gnarled trees and wildlife. If she walked to the back edge of the property, she could see the Atlantic Ocean. The briny smell sometimes wafted into the cottage itself, and Morgan swore that she could occasionally hear the waves crashing amidst the creaking of the old pine floors and the sounds of the cottage settling.

Inside, it was largely the way it had been when they were kids. Same lovingly worn floors, same beadboard walls, even much of the same furniture. They'd made a few changes to make it suitable for a shop. Morgan had set one side up to mix her herbs, Fiona the other to fashion her healing gemstone jewelry. A large counter made from old scarred wood ran along Morgan's side of the shop with an old-fashioned cash register to ring up purchases.

The holidays were fast approaching, so right now the place was decorated with lots of red bows, holly, and pine garlands, the fresh scent of which tickled Morgan's nose and complemented the gentle fall of powdery snow that dusted the branches of the pines surrounding the cottage.

Morgan turned away from the window and attempted to focus on her work. A new batch of herbs had just arrived, and she wanted to put them away in her antique apothecary chest for easy access. Currently, the bags and boxes were scattered across the big counter, where she usually mixed her poultices and ground her ingredients with the large stone mortar and pestle nearby.

Across the room, Fiona tinkered away at her long worktable, using her jewelers' tools to fashion moonstones into a new bracelet. Her long red curls hung down, pooling on the table as she bent over to work the jewels. Her sister's incessant humming of Holiday tunes would normally be welcome in early December, but today it only put Morgan further on edge.

With a sigh, she stuffed the new ingredients into the chest then got to work mixing a fresh batch of a general healing ointment. As she blended together aloe vera, peppermint, thyme, and rosemary, she did her best not to worry, all the while casting furtive glances at Fiona to try to deduce if her sister suspected her secret.

Fiona was diligently working away, seemingly oblivious to Morgan's inner turmoil, and Morgan relaxed a bit. Then she glanced at their cat, Belladonna, who sat atop an antique velvet chair as if it were her throne. Her snow-white fur reflected the scenery outside the window, and her ice-blue eyes—the same exact color that Morgan and her three sisters shared—gazed back at Morgan with a far-too-perceptive intelligence.

From the narrowed feline stare, it almost felt like Belladonna knew Morgan's inner thoughts. She frowned and pushed those thoughts aside, concentrating on her work instead.

"So, what's your take on Jolene and Mateo?" Fiona

asked about their younger sister out of the blue, jarring Morgan from her anxious thoughts.

"Uh, I think it's good," Morgan said, adding healthy helpings of chamomile, marigold, sage, and lavender to the mix. All the lovely smells wafted around her, soothing her frazzled nerves a bit. Having something else to think about besides her own problems helped too. What better topic to distract her than their love lives? All of the Blackmoore sisters had been lucky enough to find their mate. Morgan had Luke Hunter, Fiona had Jake Cooper, Celeste had Calvin Reed, and now Jolene had Mateo. "They've gotten a lot closer since the mission on Rune Island, and I for one think it's great."

"Me too," Fiona said. "Mateo's a good guy. He's saved our butts more than once."

"True. And he's obviously smitten with Jolene." Morgan ground the herbs to a fine powder then scooped in a dollop of cream to make it into an ointment. Mateo had been a bit of an enigma until just recently, seeing as how he'd just turned up randomly one day. They'd all been suspicious of him in the beginning, and rightly so. They'd been battling their archnemesis, Dr. Bly, at the time and had wondered if Mateo might've been one of his spies. He wasn't, of course, but since then, he'd proven himself to be a good guy, if still a tad mysterious. He had a tendency to leave on missions without much explanation or warning. "Good thing she got over the whole business of owing him for saving her life in Salem."

"Yeah." Fiona straightened and rolled her shoulders. She'd been bent over that worktable for at least an hour, peering through a magnifying glass as she carefully fitted each stone into its setting using a pair of tweezers. Morgan had no idea how her sister didn't end up a hunchback sometimes, or cross-eyed. Give Morgan a handful of herbs any day over a crick in her neck and a migraine from squinting too much. "I can understand her not wanting to be beholden to the guy, but I'm glad she stopped avoiding him and finally let nature take its course."

"Hmm." Morgan stirred the pulverized herbs and other ingredients together then scooped the mixture into a jar for safekeeping until it was needed. "She's stubborn though. It won't be easy for them. Jolene hates to admit her feelings."

"True. Maybe that's a good thing though. I mean, I like Mateo and all, but I still don't think they should rush into anything. She's too young to settle down. Let them take it slow." Fiona stood and stretched then walked over to her toolbox to search through the endless array of tiny screwdrivers and minuscule tools of her trade. They all looked the same to Morgan, but Fiona knew each and every one and was very particular about her tools. Which was fine, since Morgan felt the same way about her herbs. Her sisters sometimes teased her by saying she had "many flavors in her spice rack," but all the different plants had their place and their purpose. They could save lives or take them, hurt or heal, bring joy or sorrow, all depending on how they were used. Morgan loved her herbs. Or at least she *used* to.

She screwed the lid on tight to the new container of ointment then set it under her counter, joining the neat rows of other concoctions already there. With winter upon them, she'd stocked up on soothing creams for muscle strains and joint pain, knowing how the cold tended to aggravate people's arthritis. "I'm just concerned that with Mateo disappearing all the time on missions, things between them won't progress like they should. Developing a relationship means spending time together, learning about each other, sharing hopes and dreams for the future. His work makes that difficult."

Mateo Ortiz worked for the global paranormal tribunal, a group that investigated cases of otherworldly interference and abuses of power in the human world. That meant he was one of the good guys and that he was gone a lot. Jolene deserved a man who could put her first, be there when she needed him. Considering things that way, maybe Mateo wasn't the best choice for her youngest sister's mate after all. Then again, their tiny town of Noquitt, Maine, wasn't exactly crawling with eligible single guys either. Especially ones who wouldn't blink twice at a girl with some "extraordinary" abilities.

As she took her hand away from the jar of ointment, Morgan waited for the telltale tiny flicker of magic that she always got from one of her mixtures, but it didn't come. She frowned and turned away, her stomach knotting tighter.

Morgan sighed as she tidied up her counter, double-checking all the tiny drawers in her cabinet to make sure her stock was in good order. She kept them all in alphabetical order for easy tracking. Acacia, Balm of Gilead, Boneset, Chickweed, Eucalyptus. She stopped to make a note to order more of that one. Lavender, Peppermint, Rose.

The work calmed her and helped her refocus. She willed her thoughts back to Jolene and Mateo, but soon that turned into thoughts of their missions, which ratcheted up her anxiety again. The missions were the reason that Morgan was all worked up. The reason for her secret. Because on those missions, the sisters often had to use their paranormal gifts to fight enemy paranormals. Like the last mission to Rune Island. It had been successful but not because of Morgan. Because that was when she'd felt her powers starting to weaken. She'd been no help at all, but luckily her brand of intuition and herbal healing hadn't been called on much and her sisters hadn't noticed. At the time, she'd hoped it was just temporary, like a cold or the flu, and her powers would return. But that was months ago, and if anything, she felt even less powerful now.

Please don't let it be permanent. She closed her eyes and whispered the silent prayer to the heavens. Her sisters depended on her when they were called into danger to help the world of the paranormals.

They worked as a four-person team, and her gift of intuition was critical in helping them anticipate the enemy's next move. The last thing she wanted was to put them in any danger. And if her sisters found out, she was terrified they'd be disappointed in her. She was the oldest and should set an example, be a leader. Without her gifts, she couldn't do either.

Worse, she never wanted to be labeled the "useless one." She still had a lot of years left. Thirty-five was hardly decrepit, but still. With a fourteen-year gap between her and Jolene, she sometimes felt more like a surrogate mother than a sister.

Belladonna jumped down off the chair and wandered over to Morgan, twining about her ankles and sticking close to her side. The cat had been doing that a lot lately, which was strange, almost like she was trying to tell Morgan something or comfort her in her time of need. Like the feline knew there was something wrong with her, that something was happening inside Morgan, something bad. Or maybe Belladonna was scared

Morgan would screw up and wanted to be there to pick up the slack. Whatever it was, she'd always secretly suspected there was more to Belladonna than just a normal house cat. It couldn't be just coincidence that the cat shared the exact same eye color as the sisters, right?

Morgan finished making her list of supplies for reorder then began straightening the display shelves in the store. With winter on their doorstep, they didn't get as many patrons as they did in the busy summer tourist season, but still. People depended on her remedies for all sorts of things. She and Fiona had built a reputation in the natural healing community because their products were extremely powerful due to their unique gifts. Even people who didn't believe in paranormal powers made special trips to their store. People came from far and wide to purchase her herbal wares because of their potency. Of course now that her gifts were gone, who knew how potent they'd be?

As she fiddled with jars and polished the display cases where Fiona's jewelry sparkled in the front windows, Morgan couldn't help wishing she had someone to talk to about all this. But she couldn't risk telling anyone. If word got back to her sisters, that would not be good. Sure, they would be kind and understanding, but Morgan wouldn't be able to stand the looks of pity that would inevitably come.

In her desperation to find out what was wrong, she'd

even tried visiting the local paranormal healer, Clementine Vega, sneaking out of the shop the day before when Fiona had had a morning appointment.

Morgan was just about to go in the back to get another couple of jars for new ointments for one of the displays when the front door of the shop opened, and in walked Sheriff Donna White. A tall, sturdy woman, she was scowling, as usual, from beneath the brim of her hat. At least she was marginally better than the last sheriff they'd had, though. Sheriff Overton had had a vendetta against the Blackmoore sisters for reasons unknown, but as far as Morgan knew, Donna White had no beef with them. Until today, apparently, if her dour expression was any indication.

"What can we do for you today, Sheriff?" Fiona asked, looking up from her work.

"I think you know," Sheriff White said, tone as brisk as the freezing air outside.

Fiona gave her a flat look, her tone snarky. "Sorry. Nope. How about an amulet? Or maybe some chamomile poultice to help loosen you up a bit? I think Morgan just got in some fresh St. John's wort. Hear that's great for fixing crappy attitudes."

Sheriff White glared at Fiona for a second before fixing her attention on Morgan. "I don't want any of your questionable goods. I'm here to interview a person of interest."

"Person of interest?" Morgan scrunched her nose. "Interest in what?"

Fiona frowned and walked over to stand beside her sister. "Yeah. In what?"

Sheriff White gave them both a disparaging glance. "In the murder of Clementine Vega, that's what. She was killed yesterday. I've got witnesses who say they saw Morgan's beat-up old Toyota at the scene of the crime."

* * *

MORGAN'S CHEST SQUEEZED TIGHT, and she gripped the edge of the counter to keep from passing out. Clementine. The healer she'd gone to see the day before on the sly. Dead. Oh, that wasn't good at all.

"Wait a minute!" Fiona moved to stand between the sheriff and Morgan. "I'm sure my sister had nothing to do with that. Why don't you tell us exactly what happened?"

"And why doesn't your sister tell me exactly what she was doing there?" Sheriff White countered.

"She wasn't there," Fiona said before Morgan could answer. "She was here at the shop. All day. Working." She turned and glanced over her shoulder at Morgan. "Right?"

Stuck between a rock and a hard place, Morgan nodded. "Yes. I was here at the shop."

11

If she let slip that she'd closed the place and made an emergency visit to the healer, then she'd have to explain why, and she wasn't ready to go there. Not yet. Maybe not ever. Besides, Sheriff White couldn't be doing more than grasping at straws. When Morgan had left Clementine's place yesterday, the woman had still been alive and fine.

"That so?" Sheriff White asked, her tone skeptical. "Anyone around here who can vouch for your where-abouts? Customers perhaps?"

"No." Morgan's shoulders slumped slightly. "It was slow yesterday. Only a few people came in after Fiona left. Not locals either. Tourists I think. I'd never seen them before."

Belladonna sniffed around the sheriff's ankles, rubbing lightly against her, leaving a trail of white hair stuck to the woman's dark-brown uniform pants. If she hadn't been so nervous, Morgan would've chuckled at her cat's rudeness. Go Belladonna.

"It doesn't matter if no one can vouch for her being here at the shop," Fiona said, continuing to defend her sister. "Morgan's got no reason to kill Clementine. They barely know each other."

"People do all sorts of crazy things for all sorts of crazy reasons." Sheriff White scowled down at the cat hair on the hem of her uniform pants. "Hey, cut that out. I just had these things dry cleaned."

Belladonna blinked up at the sheriff with innocent

eyes, and Morgan could have sworn she saw a flicker of a smile tug at Sheriff White's lips. Go figure, the sheriff was human after all, and she liked cats. Of course only the most hard of hearts could resist Belladonna's cute face.

But then the sheriff's face hardened, and she glanced up, pinning Morgan in place with her gaze as Fiona scooped up Belladonna into her arms. "Are you accusing my sister of murder?"

"Not yet." Sheriff White gave a small, mirthless smile. "Like I said, she's a person of interest."

"Just because someone said they saw a Toyota parked out in front of Clementine's house?" Fiona snorted. "Plenty of people own old Toyotas these days."

"True." The sheriff's smile widened a bit. "But not many people have been accused of murder before, like Morgan here. Have they?"

The vise grip on Morgan's chest tightened even further. Yes, she had been, but those charges had been false. Drummed up by Sheriff Overton. The real killer had eventually been caught. Morgan had never killed anyone in her life—well, unless you counted those evil paranormals on their missions. But they deserved it.

"That's crazy! Sheriff Overton—" Fiona started before Sheriff White cut her off.

"Save your breath. I checked the records, and I know what happened back then. But I still say you girls aren't as innocent as you seem. I intend to prove that for myself."

"You can't prove anything. And maybe you should have looked a little harder," Fiona continued, not backing down an inch. "Morgan didn't kill anyone. Those accusations were false. There's a lot of beat-up Toyotas in this town. I suggest you start finding them."

"Oh, I intend to." Sheriff White headed back to the front door and opened it before turning back toward them. "You better hope there's another vehicle out there that matches the witness's description too. Because this won't be like the last time you were accused, Morgan Blackmoore." She glanced at Fiona and sneered. "Your sister won't be able to take up with one of our police officers to get you out of trouble this time." Sheriff White tipped her hat and opened the door, letting in a blast of frigid air. "You ladies take care now."

With that, Sheriff White walked out of the shop, leaving Morgan and Fiona to stare after her.

CHAPTER TWO

"Can you believe the nerve of that woman? Just because I date Jake does not mean that's why Morgan wasn't charged with murder," Fiona said, her tone indignant.

The Blackmoores had congregated in the cozy sitting room off the kitchen after dinner that night. A fire crackled in the old brick fireplace, which was about the only indication that the house was three centuries old.

Though most of the house had its original antique charm and was loaded with furniture from generations past, Morgan's mother, Johanna, had decorated this room in a more beach-modern decor. Overstuffed furniture, sky-blue throw pillows, and muted colors made it cozy and comfortable. Giant starfish and other sea-themed accents made it reminiscent of summer. A stark contrast to the howling wind and snow swirling against the window panes. Sounded like another nor'easter was blowing in. The beams in the three-hundred-year-old roof creaked under the onslaught. One of the hazards of living on a cliff above the Atlantic Ocean in Maine: the weather could be harsh in winter.

"I'm beginning to think the new sheriff's no improvement at all over the last one," Celeste said from where she was sitting on the sofa beside their mother. Her short blond hair was still damp from having spent the afternoon outside shoveling, and her cheeks were red. Her ice-blue eyes flashed with agreement at Fiona's indignation.

"Yeah, we need to watch her," Jolene said, curled in her overstuffed chair, her long brown hair cascading over one shoulder, thick pink fuzzy socks on her feet.

"This tea is delicious, dear," their mother said to Morgan, her amber eyes sparkling. She was the only Blackmoore without blue eyes, as those came from the girls' father's side. There was no evidence of the white in her long ebony hair that had been there when they'd first recovered her from a remote island after she'd been presumed dead for years. The time at home, here in Noquitt, had restored her energy and her zest for life. "Blackberry, yes?"

"Yes," Morgan said, taking a sip from her own mug. The fruity fragrance wafted around her, helping to soothe her frayed nerves. She tried to focus on the

16

conversation, but her attention kept straying to Belladonna, who'd continued to watch her with an accusing glare. "I picked the berries from the garden last summer and dried them for the tea. I'm glad you like it."

Despite the bright fruity flavor on her tongue, Morgan's stomach still knotted with guilt over how she'd lied to Fiona and Sheriff White earlier. She wished they would change the subject so she didn't have to continue to do more of the same to the rest of her family, but no such luck.

Morgan snuggled down beneath her blanket and consoled herself with the knowledge that she couldn't dare tell them the truth—that she had been at Clementine Vega's yesterday. Besides, the time for confession had passed, walking right out the door with Sheriff White earlier. If she changed her story now, it would only make things worse. Best to let everything blow over, which it would once the real killer was found.

"Poor, poor Clementine," their mother said, shaking her head. "Such an awful thing."

"Hmm," Celeste said. "She was one of the few people I felt like I'd actually gotten to know around here. Good lady. Fun tarot readings."

"Yeah," Morgan said, hoping her response would deflect attention away from her. In truth, Clementine Vega was one of the more welcoming souls within the small paranormal circle in Noquitt, Maine. They were a tight-knit community that kept to themselves, for obvious reasons. The sisters hadn't even known there was such a community, much less who was in it. Newcomers were met with suspicion until they were proven worthy. And while the Blackmoore sisters weren't newcomers to the town, they had just started believing in their own powers, and therefore, the paranormal community was just starting to reach out to them as equals.

Morgan looked up to find everyone watching her expectantly. Shoot. They must've asked her something, and she'd missed it. Unsure what to say, she went with the last known topic. Clementine. "It's too bad. She was the only magical healer in the county."

To regular folks in town, Clementine Vega had appeared to be a fiftysomething fortune teller and reiki healer. To the paranormal community, however, she'd been the one they'd sought out to help them heal supernatural issues. Speaking of that...

Celeste frowned. "You don't think this has anything to do with Dr. Bly, do you?"

The sisters all exchanged a look.

"Maybe we should look into that," Jolene suggested.

Fiona shrugged. "Then again, it could just be a regular murder."

"Yes, it probably is," Morgan agreed, perhaps too quickly in her haste to steer her siblings away from any paranormal involvement. The last thing she needed was for her sisters to look into the paranormal motives. "Let the police handle it. People do get killed for regular reasons, too, and Clementine did readings for lots of people."

"That's probably true, but one can never be too careful when it comes to Bly," Johanna chimed in. "The guys should be here soon. Maybe they'll know something about what happened to Clementine."

"The guys" consisted of Luke, Mateo, and Jake. Jake Cooper was Fiona's boyfriend and used to work for the sheriff's department—thus Sheriff White's snide comment earlier. Now he ran the local detective agency where Jolene worked. Calvin Reed, Celeste's boyfriend, was the fourth member of "the guys," and he was an antiques dealer and ran the local pawnshop. He wouldn't be there that night though since he was out of town on a buying trip.

Luke Hunter was Morgan's boyfriend, and he worked for the same secret government agency that hired the sisters to help fight in their paranormal battles. Funny how that had worked out. They'd dated in high school, years earlier, then he'd gone off to the military, and she'd stayed home in Noquitt. They hadn't seen each other again until he'd returned to town to try and recruit Morgan and her sisters for his government agency because of their skills. Now, she and Luke were right back where they'd left off prior to their high school breakup—well, if you didn't count all the magical gifts that Morgan hadn't known she'd had back then and the fact they were both quite a bit older and a whole lot wiser.

Still, if the paranormal community was involved in Clementine's murder, Luke would know about it. And if a paranormal was responsible, then hopefully he and his agency would soon unmask the true killer, and everyone would forget about Sheriff White's witness statements saying that Morgan's truck had been seen at Clementine's house.

Paranormal involvement was a double-edged sword though, given that if there were supernatural shenanigans at play, then the sisters might end up corralled into the fight against the bad guys, and with Morgan's powers still on the fritz, she might not be able to help.

Her heart lurched. It was her worst nightmare. Her sisters in peril and Morgan helpless to save them. Clementine's words from the day before repeated in her head...

You have strayed from your core. Your gifts are not to be taken lightly.

Morgan had no idea what that meant, but Clementine had promised to work out a solution for her, some steps she could take to get her gifts back. Steps she'd never get now because those instructions had died along with poor Clementine.

The front door opening announced "the guys'" arrival. Over the past year, Johanna had insisted they simply walk in. They visited often enough, and Johanna was probably sick of having to answer the door every time they came over. Morgan heard the rustle of coats being hung on the coat rack and the thudding of boots being placed in the boot tray, and then Luke and Jake appeared in the doorway.

"Hey, everyone," Jake said as he took a seat beside Fiona.

Luke shook the snow from his hair, his cheeks and nose red from the cold. He sat on the arm of Morgan's chair, leaning in to give her a quick kiss before glancing over at Jolene. "Mateo's finishing up a phone call. He'll be in in a sec."

Jolene shrugged, pretending like she didn't care as she started picking up the mugs and small plates they'd used for snacks to take into the kitchen. Morgan didn't need her intuition to tell her that Jolene cared about where Mateo was and what he was doing a lot more than she let on.

"Any new assignments from Dorian Hall?" Johanna asked from across the coffee table. Dorian Hall was Luke's contact in the agency and the one who usually doled out their assignments.

"Nope." Luke draped his arm across the back of Morgan's chair. She resisted the urge to snuggle into his heat as she sipped her tea. Best to keep a clear head during this conversation, and cuddling with Luke was endlessly distracting. "Everything's quiet around here right now. In fact, last I heard, Dr. Bly's focusing on something in China. Why?"

Fiona proceeded to tell him all about their visit from Sheriff White today while Morgan took a deep breath and forced her tense muscles to relax, even as Luke's frown deepened to a scowl. His hand dropped from the back of her chair to her shoulder in a show of solidarity.

"The sheriff all but accused Morgan of the crime just because a witness said they saw an old Toyota there," Fiona said, her voice edged with outrage as she looked at Jake beside her. "Can you believe that?"

"From our stellar local sheriff's department? You bet," Jake scoffed. "And that's flimsy evidence if I've ever heard it. There have got to be hundreds, if not thousands, of beat-up old Toyotas in this area. Sheriff White can't possibly think she has a chance of making an arrest on that alone. It could have been anyone driving that vehicle. Did she mention anything else that specifically linked Morgan to the murder?"

"No. Of course not." Morgan scowled at him. Jake had been a cop during the last time she'd been accused of killing someone. That's how he and Fiona had met.

Morgan had been innocent that time, too, but somehow these situations kept plaguing her. Ugh. She could be in real trouble if Sheriff White wanted to pursue this. She'd inadvertently left evidence behind—fingerprints, hair—that could directly link her to Clementine's house. "We just seem to be her favorite target."

"Hey," Jolene called, poking her head in from the kitchen. "You guys want some coffee while I'm up?"

At Luke and Jake's nods, she disappeared back into the kitchen. Morgan could hear her getting mugs out of the cabinets as she yelled out, "Jake, if you want, I can look up all the red Toyotas registered with the DMV in our county. See if anything comes up that's close to the year and make of Morgan's car. If so, we can take it to Sheriff White as proof it could've been someone other than my sister's car that witness saw yesterday. I'm caught up on everything, and I've got plenty of time to look things up. The only case we're working on right now is the nightly mystery noises coming from Mrs. Tower's shed on River Road."

"Look what things up?" Mateo asked, walking into the room. His hair glistened from the melted snow, and he shook himself, sending droplets everywhere. Jolene came back from the kitchen with steaming mugs, and her face brightened at the sight of him. Morgan bit back a smile. Her sister might pretend that whatever was happening between her and Mateo was no big deal, but

Morgan recognized that special glow when she saw it. It was the same glow she saw in the mirror each time she thought about Luke. She was glad her sister had found someone special.

Jolene proceeded to fill Mateo in on what had happened to Clementine and the sheriff's visit to Sticks and Stones earlier as she handed out the coffee then went back to get Mateo a mug.

"Wow, I don't know if I would write this off as a normal killing so fast," Mateo said, his expression concerned as he took the mug from Jolene. "The fact Clementine was paranormal means we can't rule out one of our own killing her. Maybe not Dr. Bly, since he's in China, but someone else. His absence shouldn't lull us into a false sense of security. We still need to be vigilant about what happens here in Noquitt."

"I think it's better that you girls be prepared, just in case," Johanna said. "And it won't hurt to have Jolene do a bit of recon."

Jake nodded. "Fine. Maybe we can go out to Clementine's place tomorrow and look around. Between Jolene's gifts with auras and Morgan's intuition, they should be able to sense any lingering evil paranormal energy there. That way we'll know what we're up against. I'll make sure to find out when the police will be done."

"I'm down for that," Jolene said eagerly.

"Me too." Morgan forced a smile. Fat lot of good her

intuition would do her, but of course she couldn't let her sisters know that. If they wanted to check out Clementine's, she'd have to go along and pretend like she just wasn't feeling any vibes. Hopefully no enemy paranormals would be there, because the last thing she needed was to end up in some sort of fight. And hopefully, they'd go during the day. Less chance of danger then, right? "Let's do it."

"Cool." Jake pulled Fiona closer to his side. "I'll check with my old contacts at the sheriff's department first thing in the morning and see what I can find out about when the crime scene will be cleared. Safer for us to check it out when we know we won't be caught breaking in by the cops. That probably wouldn't help Morgan any. I'll let everyone know."

"Let me just see if I can delay my next trip as well," Mateo said, pulling out his cell phone and typing in a text. "I was supposed to leave for China in the morning for a recon mission on what Bly's been up to over there."

"Oh, I hope you can. In the meantime, we'll do what we can to get ready here." Jolene clutched the obsidian amulet around her neck. It was identical to the one each of the Blackmoore sisters wore. They had been made by Fiona and imbued with magic to ward off evil energy. Jolene frowned at Morgan. "Where's your amulet?"

Reflexively her hand went to her neck as her

stomach went into freefall. Oh no! How could she have forgotten?

A jolt of panic zinged through Morgan. She'd taken it off yesterday per Clementine's request and put it in a dish of Himalayan sea salt to soak during her appointment. The cleansing was supposedly part of the process of reconnecting with her gifts. She was supposed to pick it up tomorrow. Her mind raced along with her pulse. She had to get it back before her sisters saw it. They'd recognize it right away.

She forced out another lie. "I, uh, must've forgotten to put it back on after my shower. It's still upstairs."

Jolene and the others gave her an odd look but thankfully let it drop.

Things were going from bad to worse. Now, Morgan not only had to figure out what was wrong with her gifts and a way to get them back, she also had to find a way to get her amulet before her sisters went in there and saw it or the sheriff picked it up as more evidence that Morgan had committed the crime.

There was only one way to do that. She was going to have to break into Clementine's before her sisters did.

CHAPTER THREE

*I*n a daze, Morgan followed Jolene back into the kitchen to help divide up the dinner leftovers for the guys while their group continued to discuss the absurdity of Sheriff White thinking Morgan's car had been at Clementine's place. She felt hot and sick and jumpy as all get out. At least if she kept busy, the guilt wasn't quite so overwhelming. She divided up the food silently, her mind whirling on how she could get into Clementine's place before everyone else and avoid the police if it was an ongoing crime scene.

"Hey," Fiona said, sticking her head into the kitchen and scaring Morgan half to death. "Jake and I are going to take off. We're meeting some friends in town."

"Okay," Jolene said, handing her sister Jake's bag of goodies. "Be careful out there. The roads are probably bad."

"And I'm going to the family library to practice," Celeste said. "Put Cal's stuff in the fridge. I'll give it to him tomorrow when he gets back."

"Done," Jolene said. "Have fun practicing."

Morgan stared after Celeste as she headed into the hallway on her way to the south side of the house where the library was. She hadn't paid much attention before, but now that she thought about it, Celeste was always hanging out in the family library, meditating and doing yoga. Well, at least Morgan assumed that was what she was doing. Had she been practicing her craft this whole time? And what did that entail? Maybe it would be a good idea to find out.

"And I'm turning in for the night," Johanna said. "I still get tired pretty early."

Morgan gave her mother a kiss then waved as she disappeared down the hall. Good, everyone was taking off. Morgan wanted to check out what Celeste was up to, and she needed time alone to formulate her plan. Now if she could just figure out how to get rid of Luke.

Mateo wandered into the kitchen and started digging through his food for a snack. Morgan took that as her clue to leave and headed back into the living room, where Luke now sat alone. Well, alone except for Belladonna, who was snuggled up beside him in the chair. The feline was still giving Morgan the stink eye, and she knew why. Because she kept digging herself deeper and deeper into trouble with all her deceptions.

"You okay?" Luke patted the cushion beside him in invitation. "You seem a bit down tonight. You aren't letting all that mess with Sheriff White get to you, I hope. We'll figure it out. I promise."

She slid beneath his arm and rested her head atop his warm, hard chest as he kissed the top of her head. The reassuring thump of his heartbeat rumbled beneath her ear. "No. It's not that." She gave a sigh followed by a small fake cough. "I think maybe I'm coming down with a cold."

Ugh. Add another lie to the ever-growing list.

Belladonna gave a disapproving meow.

"Aw." Luke placed his palm against her forehead then leaned down to kiss it gently. "Off to bed early with you then. I won't have you getting sick. I can't afford to get sick either. Go upstairs and get into bed. I'll bring you up a hot toddy."

Morgan straightened, glad her long black hair hid her flaming hot cheeks. "I'm not that sick. Seriously. If anything, it's just sniffles. I'm fine."

The cat got up and jumped over to the coffee table right in front of Morgan, gaze narrowed. Feline judgment glittered in her eyes and radiated off her small body in waves.

Wait.

If Morgan felt Belladonna's emotions, did that mean she was getting her intuition back?

"Look," Luke said, gesturing toward Belladonna. "Even Belladonna thinks you're making a bad decision. If that glare isn't dripping with disdain, I don't know what is. Just let me take care of you for once."

Morgan's shoulders drooped with disappointment. Not her intuition then, if it was obvious to Luke too. Darn.

"Hey," Mateo said, coming back into the room, his words slightly muffled by his mouthful of food. "You guys want to play some poker? Henry Drake down the street is trying to scare up a game. Jolene and I are going."

"I don't know," Luke eyed Morgan. "Morgan isn't feeling good, and I want to make sure she doesn't overdo it."

"I'm fine, really. But you go ahead and play, Luke." Morgan gave him a peck on the cheek and got up. "I'm going to turn in early. Ward off this cold before it starts."

Luke gave her an uncertain look, and she shooed him away with her hands. "Go, really. It's easier to rest if you're not hovering over me."

Luke stood. "Okay, I guess you have a point."

Perfect. Now Morgan could head to the library to see exactly what Celeste was doing to practice. Maybe that's what Clementine had in mind when she told Morgan she had to nurture her gifts. Truth was that Morgan never really did much to strengthen them. They'd always just sort of been there. Was that why they were failing her now? Was it as simple as doing some exercises to get them back? But what exercises? Morgan had no idea, but if she could see what Celeste was doing, maybe she could do something similar.

After she checked out what Celeste was doing, she could have some alone time to think about the best way to get to Clementine's place before her sisters tomorrow.

She said her goodnights, kissed Luke goodbye, and promised to call him in the morning to let him know how she was, then headed over to the south side of the huge mansion. They built them big and sturdy three centuries ago, and Blackmoore House had stood the test of time. The library was a regal room with jewel-toned oriental rugs on the floor and oak bookcases that soared ten feet high to the ceiling around the perimeter of the space. Expanses of burgundy papered walls, broken by paintings of old ancestors in gold-gilt frames.

Celeste was sitting in the middle of the room on one of the rugs when Morgan arrived. A book was open in front of her, but her eyes were closed in concentration. Morgan hesitated in the doorway to watch as the pages flipped slowly on their own.

"Don't just stand there," Celeste said without opening her eyes, making Morgan jump. "Come on in."

Great. Seemed even her sister had better intuition than Morgan these days. "What are you doing?" she asked as she took a seat on the rug across from Celeste.

"Like I said, I'm practicing." More pages of the book flipped on their own. "Ever since I discovered I could cast spells when we went to Salem, I've been trying to up my game. So far, all I've been able to do is minor things, like turning these pages with a simple spell and some focused concentration, but it's still something, and I don't want to lose the ability."

She peeked one eye open to glance at Morgan. The pages stopped turning, then she opened both eyes with a sigh. "We have to nurture our gifts, you know. Just like you nurture those plants and herbs of yours. If you don't give them fertilizer, sunshine, and water, they'll wither away and die. Same with our gifts. If we don't train and practice and keep improving them, they'll go away."

Morgan's chest squeezed tight. That was eerily similar to what Clementine had been trying to tell her. Could these exercises of Celeste's be the cure to what ailed her?

"I mean my skills aren't anywhere near as important as yours," Celeste continued. "But I still want them to be the best they can be."

"Your gifts are just as important as mine," Morgan scoffed. "You can see ghosts, for goodness sake. Talk to them and find out what they know. That's helped us tremendously."

"Yeah, but you can't rely on ghosts. They never show up when we need them."

"Do you think maybe Clementine's ghost will appear? She could tell us what happened." Morgan tried to tamp down the rush of hope that idea brought and failed. Having Clementine speak to them from beyond the grave and reveal the name of her killer would certainly solve the majority of Morgan's problems at the moment. Unless, of course, Clementine's ghost also blabbed to everyone that Morgan had been at her place on the day she'd died.

Celeste shrugged. "Maybe. But if paranormals are involved in the murder, we're going to need your intuition more."

True. Normally, when the sisters were about to be attacked, Morgan could feel it ahead of time. She could also ascertain the moves their opponents would make. Sometimes she could tell where people had been or if they were hiding when they walked into a room. But with her gifts basically nonexistent at present, those talents wouldn't help them. Not until she figured out what was wrong.

"Too bad about Sheriff White having it out for us too. I hoped we'd put all that behind us once Overton was gone." Celeste leaned back on her hands. "White seems just as bad though, at least from what she said to you. How dare she accuse an innocent person like that, with no proof at all. And in your shop too. Good thing no customers were in there. Could be bad for business."

Morgan nodded but didn't say anything, too caught up in trying to figure out how she was going to get into Clementine's house to get back her amulet without anyone knowing.

"I wouldn't worry about it though." Celeste smiled. It took Morgan a moment to realize she was still talking about Sheriff White and not Morgan breaking into a crime scene. "Like Jake said, there's a ton of Toyotas out there, and we all know you had nothing to do with Clementine's death. The real culprit will turn up soon enough."

Her sister sat forward again and closed her eyes to concentrate on her practicing, and Morgan stared at the book. The pages started flipping again, rhythmically, hypnotically. Practice and nurture. Practice and nurture. Practice and nurture.

But how could she practice and nurture her own gifts? It wasn't like there were intuition exercises that would show results like the flipping of pages in a book. And how would she know if it was working?

Celeste squinted sideways at Morgan. "I cast spells, and you can see the results because the pages flip. But your gift of intuition is a bit different." Stunned, Morgan just blinked at her sister. How had Celeste known what Morgan was thinking? Was it just a coincidence? As far as she knew, none of them could read minds. Not yet anyway. But she'd have to be more on guard in the future, just in case.

"Like with your herbs," Celeste continued, her blond hair glistening gold in the candle light. "You can make your concoctions and test them out on your clients and see the results. Intuition is a way different animal. I guess it's not as easy for you to practice, is it?"

Morgan shook her head.

"Meow."

Morgan looked over her shoulder to find Belladonna standing in the doorway of the library, rubbing her cheek against the doorframe. A new idea occurred. Testing her gifts on humans under the current circumstances was tricky, but Morgan had always felt connected emotionally to the feline. Perhaps she could use the cat to test out her intuition. If what had transpired downstairs was any indication, Belladonna already suspected something was wrong. Cats were way smarter than people gave them credit for, and Belladonna was more intelligent than most. And there was no way she could tell her sisters what was up.

Perfect.

She got up and started out of the room, scooping the cat up on the way. "Have fun practicing."

Celeste simply nodded then closed her eyes, focusing again on the book. Silently, Morgan left the library and headed for her own room. She'd spend some time working with the cat, trying to pick up her emotions with her intuition, then figure out how to get into Clementine's place to retrieve her amulet.

CHAPTER FOUR

*T*he next day, Morgan was up early. Her plan was to sneak out of the house before anyone else was awake. She hoped to get to Clementine's place before the police started their day and before her sisters arrived. Plus, she was scheduled to work at Sticks and Stones first thing, and Fiona would get suspicious if she showed up late. Just to be on the safe side, she left a note in the kitchen telling Fiona she was stopping to pick up coffees on the way to work. Then she slipped outside and hurried to her truck.

She parked a few blocks away from Clementine's house, not wanting any nosy neighbors to spot her there again. Morgan climbed out and turned to lock the doors, only to hear a loud meow from inside the vehicle.

Great. Belladonna had snuck into the car again.

There was no time to take her back to the house now,

and it wouldn't have done any good anyway. The cat never stayed where she was supposed to. It was too cold to leave her in the car, so Morgan had no choice but to unlock the door and let her come along. On second thought, it could turn out to be a good thing, she supposed. Given her lack of intuition, the feline's senses could be helpful. She reached in and pulled out the cat, tucking her safely inside her coat for warmth, then locked up and headed toward Clementine's place.

Police tape still covered the doors and windows from what she could see from the road, but there weren't any officers in sight, thank goodness. Several rows of footprints tracked through the snow. Morgan double-checked to make sure no one was around then carefully picked her way through the existing tracks to avoid leaving any new footprints for the cops to find. The street was quiet, especially this early, and Clementine's house was set away from the others anyway. The sun had barely started to rise, the sky streaked with bands of red and gold near the horizon. Her breath frosted on the wind, and Belladonna squirmed inside her down coat. Maybe she should consider taking the cat more places in winter. She was hot in there, like a little mini space heater.

In fact, she'd not noticed the other day, but there really were no other houses in the vicinity besides Clementine's. A gigantic oak tree and some smaller elms stood to the far left of the lot, and Morgan could see a small red ranch house a little ways away. Oh right, that was Alma Myers's place. Honestly, in the summer, with all the leaves on the trees, the other house probably wouldn't be visible at all, but now, with the limbs bare, the nearest neighbor would have a limited view of Clementine's property.

The windows of Alma's house were dark though, from what Morgan could see, meaning she was either still asleep or not home. Good. And it wasn't like she had a choice about breaking and entering or not. She had to get her amulet back, especially since her sisters were planning on coming here.

Traipsing through the snow along the side of the house to the rear yard, Morgan hesitated at the back door. If Celeste was here, she could unlock it with one of her spells, but even when they were working properly, Morgan's gifts didn't include that kind of magic. Good thing Jolene had taught her how to pick a lock the old-fashioned way. Another bonus of working at a PI's office.

Morgan crouched and pulled out the small leather pouch that Jolene had given her with everything she needed to break any type of lock. She pulled off her gloves, blowing on her fingers to keep them warm and flexible, before picking up the tiny, delicate tools.

Belladonna meowed from inside her coat, poking her head out the top of the zipper to watch. The last thing she needed was her fingerprints on the door, so easy did

39

it, even if her prints were probably all over the house already. Thoughts of Sheriff White pulling up to the front of the Blackmoore House, lights blazing, to arrest Morgan flashed through her head.

Nope. Not going there. She forced herself to concentrate on picking the lock instead. Given that the temperatures had dropped to almost zero last night, she and Belladonna would get frostbite if they stayed out here much longer.

Morgan blew on her stiff fingers again then got to work, slipping two picks into the lock to align the tumblers just so. A few clicks later and she smiled as the door creaked open. She packed up her tools and pulled her gloves back on before heading inside and quietly closing the door behind her.

The quiet stillness inside the house was a bit creepy, so different from the lively surroundings of the day before when she'd had her appointment with Clementine. Then, there'd been soothing new-age music playing in the background and sweet patchouli incense burning. Candles had been lit, and bright winter sunshine had filled the place. And Clementine had still been alive.

Now the place was as silent as a funeral parlor and smelled like death.

She took a moment of silence in reverence to the woman who'd died here then slowly proceeded farther into the house. Belladonna meowed loudly from inside her coat, so she slowly unzipped and unloaded the feline, placing her down on the ground to explore. From the police markers, it appeared Clementine had been murdered in the kitchen, at the table. The remnants of a body outline were still on the floor. One of the chairs was pulled out, and the table was still set with a teapot. No plates or cups though. That was weird. Then again, perhaps the police had already taken them into custody as evidence. As murder scenes went, it was pretty neat and orderly. Apparently there hadn't been much of a struggle. No strange burn marks on the floor or walls or other abnormalities that indicated murderous para-normal energy.

It was chilly in the house, though at least there was no wind. The sound of the breeze whistling past lent a more sinister air to the house than Morgan remembered. Her mind raced as she walked from the kitchen into the living room. Clementine had told her during her appointment that she only brought clients into her front parlor, never farther. Could that mean the killer was someone Clementine knew, then? The fact she'd been murdered in the kitchen certainly suggested that.

As Morgan peered around the place, she tried to summon her intuition to divine a solution but got noth-ing. Belladonna trotted past Morgan's booted feet, sniffing everything and watching Morgan carefully. The wind howled louder outside and spurred her onward.

There was no time to inspect the rest of the house now. She needed to get her amulet from the parlor and get out of here.

She crept into the front room and opened the glass door cabinet where Clementine kept her dishes of sea salt. There it was!

Morgan's heart leapt at the sight of her black obsidian stone resting inside a purple dish. Beside the dish with her amulet were a set of china teacups. Clementine had used one of them to read Morgan's tea leaves the day before. The pattern matched the teapot in the kitchen.

Two of the cups, Morgan noticed, were set rim-side down, their handles perfectly aligned. A third one sat with them, rim-side up. Odd, that one would be different. Then again, she didn't know Clementine that well. Just because Morgan was a neatnik who liked everything in order didn't mean everyone else was like that too. Maybe Clementine just didn't care, or maybe she'd been in a hurry. Or perhaps she'd been drinking tea with her assailant in the kitchen and the police had put the cups back after processing them. That would explain the absence of cups in the kitchen and indicate that she had known her killer.

Shoving her thoughts about the teacups aside, Morgan grabbed her amulet and put it on then hurried back to the kitchen, where Belladonna was now meowing loudly.

"What's the matter?" Morgan whispered as she came around the corner to find the cat batting at something with her paw. "No, no. Don't touch anything, Belladonna. We shouldn't disturb things."

She didn't want to mess with anything at the crime scene. The police weren't done yet, at least according to the tape still covering the doors and windows. If she got caught tampering with a crime scene, Sheriff White would have a field day. Plus, most likely, they'd photographed the area too and would know if anything had been tampered with.

When Belladonna continued to bat whatever she'd found around with her paw, Morgan bent down and picked her up then noticed the object that the cat had seemed fascinated with. It appeared to be a small scrap of paper. Morgan picked it up and found it was thicker stock, almost like a business card, slightly laminated with pretty blue and purple colors on one side but no writing. Weird. There was no police marker near the paper, so it didn't appear to have been catalogued by the police. Had Belladonna brought it to Morgan as a clue?

She chuckled at her own silliness. Of course not. That wasn't possible, right? Then again, it wouldn't be the first time Belladonna had helped them out with a clue. Maybe she should take it more seriously.

As she inspected the tiny piece of paper more closely, a creak issued from the floorboards near the front door. Morgan's heart clogged her throat. Someone else was here. She scooped up the cat and stuffed the scrap of paper into her pocket.

She was just turning to escape out the back door when a figure appeared in the kitchen doorway.

CHAPTER FIVE

"**M**organ? What are you doing here?" Mateo whispered, walking into the kitchen with a confused expression. "Where's your car?"

An odd mix of relief and alarm washed over her. Yes, it was Mateo, her friend and her sister's boyfriend, not some deranged killer. But also, crap! It was Mateo. She'd have to explain to him why she was here, and her mind whirled, trying to come up with a plausible excuse for why she hadn't waited for the others.

"I, uh, I couldn't sleep, so I thought I'd get a head start." She shrugged, hoping it looked nonchalant. "Besides, since I'm the one on Sheriff White's person-of-interest list, I wanted to see for myself what was in here."

Lame, lame, lame. Hey, wait, why was Mateo here without the others? Last night it sounded like they were all going to come together, but she was sure no one else was in the house besides Mateo and herself. "And what exactly are you doing here?"

Mateo reached over to stroke Belladonna's head, and she nuzzled against his hand. He smiled at the fluffy white cat. "I talked to the tribunal about Clementine to see if they knew any paranormal reasons why someone might want her dead. They don't think the murder has any paranormal motives though, so we still have no clue what's going on."

The cat purred loudly while Mateo scratched behind her ears.

Morgan didn't miss the fact that Mateo had neatly avoided her question or the way he was avoiding eye contact.

He straightened and narrowed his gaze on her. "I thought you were coming later with your sisters."

Morgan fiddled with the hem of her scarf and tapped her booted toe against the floor, her chin raised defiantly. "I thought the same thing about you."

"I had to change my plans," he said, looking away. "Got an appointment later."

"Huh. Well, you really didn't need to come at all, honestly." Morgan exhaled slowly, forcing her tense muscles to relax, reminding herself that Mateo was on their side now, even if they'd had their doubts about him in the beginning. "My sisters and I can more than handle a simple recon mission to a crime scene."

They stood in awkward silence for a moment.

"Wait a minute!" Morgan squinted at him, frowning. "You were checking this place out on the sly, weren't you? Making sure there were no traps set for us. Did the tribunal send you here? What's going on, Mateo?"

He gave her a sheepish look. "No. I came on my own." He sighed. "Okay, fine. Yes. I just wanted to make sure things were safe before you and your sisters came in here. Is that so bad?"

"Jolene won't like it. In fact, she's gonna be pissed," Morgan said, shaking her head. Her sister had resented him enough at first for saving her, when Jolene had felt perfectly capable of saving herself. Thankfully, she'd gotten over it. No sense rocking the boat again now. "She's independent to a fault."

"Not anymore pissed than she will be when she finds out you came here alone to nose around without them," he countered, raising a brow.

Ugh. The guy had a point.

Eyeing each other, they stood with their arms crossed.

Finally, Morgan said, "Fine. I won't tell if you won't."

"Deal." Mateo gave a curt nod. "We'll keep this little visit between us."

Fresh guilt swamped Morgan's already-frazzled nerves. Add another person to her list. She hated lying to

Mateo and everyone else, but she couldn't tell them what was really going on.

"So, did you find anything?" Mateo asked, breaking her out of her thoughts.

"Uh, no." She fiddled with the scarf around her neck, confirming the amulet was still in its place, then patted her pocket where the scrap of paper was hidden. "What would I find?"

"I mean with your intuition." He gave her some serious side-eye. "Any gut feelings about what went down in here?"

"Oh, um, no. Nothing in here really." She glanced out the window, hoping her growing anxiety wasn't written all over her face. "Before I came inside, I was actually looking around to see if any of her neighbors had a car like mine." She gestured toward the pictures hanging in a row on the wall. "Or maybe if one of these people drove a Toyota. If it's not paranormally motivated, like you said, then it could be someone else she knew, a relative or friend."

"Well, whoever it was, we better get a move on." He tapped his watch. "Jake said the cops are coming back to finish up here and remove the crime scene tape at eight o'clock sharp. They're done processing evidence here, but we still shouldn't be anywhere near the premises until they're entirely gone. Especially you. That's why Jolene and the others are coming this afternoon."

48

"Right. Let's go then." The last thing Morgan needed was for Sheriff White to see her near Clementine's house, so Mateo didn't have to tell her twice. They exited through the back door, and Morgan made sure it was locked behind them. Outside, it was getting lighter as the sun rose in the sky. Based on the cloudless blue, it would be another frigid day.

They parted ways at the end of the driveway, Mateo calling to her, "Remember, we never saw each other here."

BY THE TIME Morgan had picked up the coffees and walked into Sticks and Stones, she was only a half hour late. Fiona was busy at work, as usual.

"Good morning," Morgan said, setting down Fiona's vanilla latte on her workbench then carrying her own yerba mate tea over to her counter.

"What took you so long?" Fiona asked, glancing up at her.

"The coffee shop was super busy this morning." Morgan hung her coat and hat on a peg on the wall behind her apothecary cabinet while Belladonna got settled in a chair directly across from Morgan's workspace and promptly fell asleep, probably worn out from all the snooping earlier, Morgan supposed. Just as well.

She could do without another bout of the intense feline staring right now.

"Have you gotten any new vibes about who might have killed Clementine?" Fiona asked as Morgan got out her supplies to mix her herbs for the day. Fiona was still working on her moonstone bracelet from the day before. "I know we talked about it, and he's supposed to be in China, but I still think Dr. Bly could have something to do with it."

"It's not paranormal related," Morgan said without thinking then scrambled to cover her tracks. "I mean that's not the sense I'm getting."

"Really?" Fiona straightened, gaze narrowed. "So, your intuition has given you some clues, then?"

"Nothing specific," she hedged before crouching down to pretend to search for something under her counter. She hated lying to her sisters like this, but it wasn't like she could tell them that Mateo had talked to the tribunal and he'd told her this morning they weren't suspecting paranormal involvement or that she hadn't seen any signs of paranormal fighting in the kitchen where Clementine had been killed. Besides, she and Mateo had made a deal. Morgan intended to keep it. She could only hope Mateo would too. She grabbed an empty jar and straightened, forcing what she hoped was a confident smile. "I'm thinking we probably shouldn't waste too much time looking into it."

"Huh, maybe—"

Whatever Fiona had been about to say was interrupted by a customer coming into the shop.

The woman, who looked about fifty and had been in the shop the week before, had dark circles under her eyes. She looked about as tired as Morgan felt.

"Hi," the woman said, walking up to Morgan's counter. "Remember me? I bought a bag of chamomile tea from you last week to help me sleep, but it's not working."

"Oh, dear. I'm so sorry." Morgan took the bag and receipt from her to process the refund. "Are you under a lot of stress?"

"Who isn't?"

"Okay. Maybe valerian root would be a better choice then. We could do an exchange today and see how you like it." Morgan ignored her sister's raised brow and focused on her customer instead. They'd never once had a customer return goods due to defective magic. She made sure to grab a bag of tea that had been made before her gifts went wonky. "If you're still not satisfied at that time, then we can process your refund."

The woman inspected the new bag of tea, nose wrinkled, and gave a reluctant nod. "I'm desperate, so I'll try anything at this point. I'll be back here next week though for my money if it doesn't work."

"Of course." Morgan packaged up the woman's new

purchase, her fingers trembling with worry. If her herbs were losing power, then things with her gifts were getting even worse. She handed the tea to the woman then glanced over to find Belladonna watching her again from the chair with that Sphinxlike look. Head lowered, Morgan reached into her pocket to confirm the scrap of paper she'd picked up from the floor of Clementine's home was still there, relieved to feel the paper tickle her fingertips as they slid across it.

Alone again, both sisters got back to work. It wasn't long though before Fiona was back to talking about the case. "Jake said the cops will be done at Clementine's place by this afternoon."

"Yeah?" Morgan did her best to sound like this was new information. "Okay."

"Mateo was there when Jake called, but I let Celeste and Jolene know already too. They're going to meet us here at three, and we can close a little early to head over to Clementine's at four. Hopefully we can find something." Fiona sat back to inspect her work. "Perfect timing, actually, since Mom is making a lasagna tonight. We can head to the house afterward and discuss everything."

"Luke said he was going to talk to his contacts at the agency today to see what he can find out too," Morgan said, grinding up some sage with a mortar and pestle. She could still feel the weight of Belladonna's judgmental stare on her, but she ignored it as best she could. She closed her eyes and said a silent prayer that they'd find out who the real killer was soon and that she'd get her gifts back up to full power as soon as possible. Morgan wasn't sure how much longer she could keep up with all this deception.

CHAPTER SIX

"*Nunc aperire*," Celeste murmured while holding her hand over the knob of Clementine's door that afternoon. A hush fell over the sisters as they listened for the lock to snick open. Morgan couldn't help glancing around to make sure there were no telltale signs of her visit here earlier. She and Mateo had been careful, but still.

"There."

Celeste creaked opened the door slowly and started inside before Fiona stopped her with a hand on her arm.

"Should we wait for Mateo?" Fiona whispered.

"Oh, he can't make it," Jolene said, with a flat stare and a dismissive wave. "He had a work trip again." When the others gave her an inquiring look, her cheeks pinked. "What? It's not like we can't figure this out on our own. We don't need him babysitting us all the time. I'm glad he had other plans." She pushed past Celeste and Fiona and walked inside.

Fiona snorted. "Girl always was too stubborn to admit she needs help."

"Exactly why I think Mateo's a great match for her, even if Jo's loathe to admit it," Celeste added, following Fiona through the door. "They make a good pair. Balance each other out."

Morgan was just glad the attention was on someone other than her. Not to mention the fact that perhaps Mateo wasn't as chill about all of Jolene's antics as he let on. If her sister found out he'd been here scoping out the place earlier, she'd go ballistic. One more reason to keep quiet about it all. She reached inside her coat to fiddle with her amulet then followed the others inside.

After closing the door behind them, they focused their attention on the kitchen, since it was obvious that's where Clementine had been killed. The police tape was gone, as were the yellow markers on the floor, but there was still a layer of print dust on everything, and the room smelled of antiseptic and a slight hint of death that no amount of cleaner would remove. Morgan shut her eyes, desperately trying to summon her intuition. It would be so helpful right about now and would solve all of her problems, but she got nothing back. Not even a frisson of power. Head lowered, she blinked back the sting of tears. What if she was permanently broken? What if her gifts never returned? What would she do with her life if she was just another ordinary person?

"I'm picking up some auras and energy, but it's scattered," Jolene said, jarring Morgan from her morose thoughts. "Feels like two paranormals, but from the vibes I'm getting, neither meant Clementine any ill will. Morgan, what have you got?"

The sisters turned to her for confirmation, and her stomach dropped to her toes. In the past, she'd have been ready with helpful information, eager to solve the mystery. Now she just felt ashamed and sad. With everyone counting on her though, Morgan needed to say something.

She quickly scrambled, closing her eyes and putting on a show of trying to sense her intuition. "Uh, yeah. I'm picking up two paranormals as well." Morgan figured that the two paranormal energies Jolene was picking up were most likely hers and Mateo's from earlier, but she couldn't very well say that. Better to just confirm and cast some doubt, because the last thing she wanted was to send her sisters off onto some kind of paranormal witch hunt that could put them in danger. Especially since both Mateo's and Luke's sources doubted that Clementine's death was paranormally motivated. "Um, maybe they just knew the victim? You know, paranormals do hang out together."

She'd dug this hole, and now she had to find a way

out of it. What she needed was a way to get her sisters on board with the idea that this might be a regular human-motivated killing without spilling her secret. That would put them off her scent and also focus their attentions where they were likely to do the most good.

"Hmm? They knew her, huh? Let me see if I can conjure Clementine's ghost, and she can tell us who they were." Celeste closed her eyes and murmured one of her Latin spells again, but nothing happened. "Darn. Nada. I'm sorry, but you guys know the ghosts don't always appear on command, and the paranormal spirits are especially difficult because they're less apt to be attached to the earthly plane. Poor Clementine is probably exploring her new world in the afterlife. That's bound to take up a lot of time, especially at first."

Belladonna wandered past Morgan, giving her the stink eye again, most likely for lying to her sisters once more, but what else was she supposed to do? She was in too deep and drowning faster by the second. She took a couple of deep breaths and forced the chaos inside her to calm. If she had any hope of making it through this disaster, she had to think rationally, look at the facts. Morgan had watched enough TV detective dramas to know that usually the guilty party was someone close to the person murdered. Who would've spent the most time in Clementine's orbit? Clients for one. Maybe friends, if she had any. A boyfriend, perhaps? She didn't know Clementine well and hadn't remembered seeing a ring on her finger or any pictures of a happy couple anywhere, but it was possible she was seeing someone.

Okay. That's where she should focus her attention, then, and try and steer her sisters there, too, if she could.

"Boy, the room is awfully neat for a crime scene. I don't think she struggled much," Fiona said.

Celeste pointed to the table. "And look at the teapot. She must've known her killer. Because why else would she have tea on the table?"

"She might've been serving it for a client," Jolene said. "I know she read tea leaves and also just liked to provide a relaxed homey atmosphere."

"In her kitchen? Is that where she normally served clients?" Fiona asked.

"Not sure. Do we know for sure she died in here? I mean, it looks that way with the chair and all, but maybe that was just from a struggle." Jolene dug out her phone. "I'll text Jake and see if he can get us a crime-scene picture from one of his contacts. It's a long shot, but what the heck? It would help to know just how Clementine's body was found."

Morgan bit her tongue. She knew exactly where the body had been because she'd seen the remnants of the outline. That was gone now though, and she couldn't very well tell her sisters she'd been here before the police cleaned up. She also knew that Clementine

59

normally served tea to clients in the parlor, but how could she tell her sisters that? This meant more than ever that Clementine knew who had done this to her.

They proceeded out of the kitchen and into the living room and then the front parlor. Jolene and Celeste even checked out the upstairs and the attic while Fiona and Morgan stayed on the first floor, but nothing. There were no more clues, no more energy—paranormal or otherwise.

"Well, I think from the fact that there wasn't a lot of physical damage to the house or its furnishings, we can deduce that there was no violent fight or struggle. Seems to point to her knowing her attacker as well," Jolene said. She'd recently taken several courses in investigating crime scenes for her job at Jake's PI firm in hopes of one day maybe getting out from behind her desk and assisting him on cases. "Based on what we saw in the kitchen, maybe Clementine and her mystery guest argued, and the killer had caught her by surprise with the attack. Or possibly there was no argument, and the killer came over to lull her into security before attacking from behind. If they used some kind of magic on her to restrain her, it wouldn't have been hard to do her in then."

"Maybe, but I'm beginning to lean more and more toward this not being paranormal or Dr. Bly related at all. After all, Luke told me last night that his agency has no reports of any paranormal activity here. Maybe it's best if we just let things go for now. Let the police do their work. I'm guessing it's just a normal run-of-the-mill human murder anyway. That's what my intuition's telling me." Morgan felt quite proud of herself for weaving together a bit of truth with that whopper of a lie without flinching. The fact she was getting better and better at fooling people dampened her enthusiasm though. She didn't want to be a competent liar. She wanted to get her gifts back and tell the truth again.

"Sorry, sis. But I disagree," Celeste said. "It's best we stay on top of things. Why can't we keep looking at both angles until we find the party responsible? That seems like the most prudent choice."

"Agreed," Fiona said then pointed at Morgan's neck. "Glad to see you're wearing your amulet again at least. You might need it with all this skullduggery going on. There are four of us. We should have no problem keeping both investigations going. Morgan, if you're leaning toward the human side more, then you can look into that. I'll help when I can. Jolene and Celeste, you guys can stick with the paranormal angle. Does that work for everyone?"

"Skullduggery? Seriously?" Jolene rolled her eyes. "You've been reading too many old mysteries again, haven't you? And yes, that works fine for me."

"And me," Celeste added.

Morgan just nodded, not trusting her voice at the moment. That was so not the outcome she'd been hoping for.

"Cool. Let's get going, then. There's nothing more for us to find here. Mom will have dinner ready at five, and I'm starving." Fiona headed for the door along with the rest of them.

As Morgan closed Clementine's door behind her once more, her determination grew. Whatever was causing her intuition to fail, she needed to find out and fast, before her sisters got into trouble sticking their noses where they didn't belong. She shoved her hands in her pockets and kept her head down as she trudged through the snow once more, the persistent wind making her eyes water.

They'd almost reached Celeste's vehicle when a woman in her mid-fifties hailed them. It was Alma Myers, the neighbor who lived closest to Clementine, just beyond the big oak tree. Morgan shuffled her feet to keep warm as she studied the woman. Alma and Clementine couldn't have been more opposite as far as physical characteristics. Where Clementine had been hefty, Alma was birdlike, thin, petite, and frail looking. Where Clementine had dark hair and Mediterranean olive skin and features, Alma had platinum-blond hair and icy-green eyes.

"What are you Blackmoores doing here?" Alma asked, making her way over to them, scowling.

"We just came by to pay our respects to Clementine. We usually stop by the deceased's home to sort of pay homage to them," Jolene said before anyone else could come up with a suitable excuse. Maybe Morgan wasn't the only accomplished liar in the family. "We didn't mean to disturb you."

Alma harrumphed. "Everyone disturbs me these days." She waved her hand toward Clementine's property. "First the police were here, traipsing all over the place and tracking snow everywhere, dirtying it up with mud and exhaust. I tried to keep an eye on things, keep them from making a mess of Clementine's property, even though she's dead. I hate it when things are messy."

Morgan's ears perked up at that. "You said you kept an eye on things here. Were you and Clementine close? Did you happen to see anything odd the day she died? Did she have any close friends that stopped by to see her regularly?"

"No. I wasn't home when it happened. I was at the church bake sale. We were acquaintances, yes. Being neighbors, you learn stuff about people. I wouldn't say we were friends though. In fact, I don't remember her having any close friends. Lots of clients though. Otherwise, Clementine kept to herself." She rubbed her eyes with shaking hands, visibly upset. "But like I said, I kept an eye on her when I could. It's a good thing, too, since I could've been the one killed instead of poor Clementine. We live so close, you know." She pointed at her home through the branches of the oak tree, which wasn't really all that close, at least in Morgan's opinion. In fact, things felt more than a bit isolated, as they had that morning too. Alma continued. "And if there's some maniac on the loose, killing innocent women, I need to know about it. I could be next!"

Fiona put her arm around the smaller woman's shoulders, her tone soothing. "At this point, I think you're safe, Alma. The police haven't mentioned a maniac at all. If you're that concerned, you should talk to Sheriff White about it."

"I did, thank you very much." Alma gave Fiona a withering stare. "I was one of the first people they questioned after it happened. Who do you think told them about that Toyota parked out front? Beat-up old thing probably belongs to young hooligans. That's the type of car they drive. And I talked to Sheriff White again when she was here earlier to take down the crime-scene tape. She explicitly implied that whoever did this was still out there, still a danger." She looked around nervously. "In fact, I need to get back inside now. Not safe in this neighborhood anymore."

She walked off toward her home, and the sisters stared after her.

With winter on their doorstep, the sun set earlier now, and the days were short. Wind whipped around them, and Morgan huddled inside her down coat, trying to piece together what Alma had just said with what she already knew.

She climbed into the back seat of Celeste's car, alongside Fiona, deep in thought. Sheriff White had never struck Morgan as particularly talkative, so she doubted that the sheriff had explicitly told Alma anything. Most likely she'd told Alma to get off her back instead. Then again, Alma did have a good eyeshot of Clementine's place, and it was possible that she could have seen something more than Morgan's car. And until they knew who was responsible for poor Clementine's death, it probably was wise to stay on guard.

At least Morgan knew now who'd reported her car being present to the sheriff, even if Alma hadn't connected the vehicle to Morgan specifically, thank goodness. She'd have to be more careful around the woman even as she looked deeper into what had happened to Clementine Vega.

Even though it would solve a lot of problems for Morgan, she doubted Clementine had been killed by a random stranger. No, the paranormal healer had been killed for a reason. And Morgan needed to figure out what that was fast.

CHAPTER SEVEN

*W*hile the Blackmoore sisters were busy breaking and entering, their mother had been busy making a lasagna. The delicious fragrances of garlic and baked cheese filled the foyer, and the girls wasted no time slipping out of their winter gear and heading into the kitchen.

The kitchen in the old mansion always gave Morgan that cozy feeling of home. Perhaps it was the familiarity of the lovingly worn black-and-white tile floor and the dark mahogany Victorian cabinets or maybe the smells of good food and the sight of her mother standing at the stainless steel stove. Her mother's absence in the kitchen during the time she was missing had been like a big dark hole in Morgan's life, and now it was filled again.

The kitchen was a homey mix of old and new and had been updated with modern appliances and granite counters, including an island they could all eat at. The old slate sink had been replaced with a double stainless-steel one, and the window above it had been widened for a better view of the herb garden at the top of the cliff and the ocean beyond.

They helped Johanna get everything on the table—salad, pasta, bread, wine—then they all took a seat around the island. Even Belladonna was chowing down on her cat food at her bowl. At least she had found something to do besides glare at Morgan.

"Hey, ladies," Mateo said, breezing into the kitchen and dropping a kiss on the top of Jolene's head, avoiding eye contact with Morgan. "I was just finishing up some work in the den. Sorry I can't stay for dinner. Tried to delay my trip, but I've got another new assignment. Save me the leftovers in a doggie bag, please."

He grabbed a piece of garlic bread, kissed Johanna on the cheek, and started out of the room, but Fiona stopped him. "Hey, I know Luke said there was no paranormal involvement in Clementine's death, according to his agency, but have you heard anything?"

"Nope. Sorry. Nothing that would connect her death to Dr. Bly, anyway. That's been my main focus, as of late."

Fiona forked up some lasagna. "Hmm... maybe her death had nothing to do with paranormals."

"It's kind of looking that way. Maybe you guys should

just let the police do the investigation." Mateo's gaze lingered on Jolene, who scowled at him.

"I think we can do better than Sheriff White, and besides, we need to clear Morgan," Jolene said.

Morgan's gut clenched as her other sisters nodded their agreement. Her sisters would do anything for her. But how would they feel if they knew she'd been lying to them?

Mateo simply shrugged and continued into the hall. "Be careful!"

Jolene watched him leave, her hand going to the amulet at her neck. Morgan noticed a tiny acorn pendant resting atop Jolene's amulet.

"That acorn pendant is cute. Is it new?" Anything to change the subject.

Jolene looked down at the pendants. "I found it in my jacket pocket after we left Rune Island. I had Fiona make it into a necklace for me, as a commemoration of our trip. Pretty, huh?"

Morgan reached out to inspect the necklace further. "It is. Nice job, Fiona."

As she sat back, she noticed Celeste had a small knowing smile on her face. Did she know that Morgan was feigning interest to change the subject, or was there more to that pretty acorn pendant than met the eye? Maybe more practicing of spells on her sister's part. And if that were the case, she ventured to guess the spell had something to do with Mateo.

Out in the hallway, she heard the front door opening and the sounds of Luke and Cal taking off their coats and saying hello and goodbye in passing to Mateo. A few seconds later, they came into the kitchen. Luke gave Morgan a quick kiss then filled his plate with food. "This looks great, Johanna."

"Thanks." Johanna smiled at Luke. She'd known him since they were kids, and he was almost like a son to her. In fact, Johanna was close to all their boyfriends, especially Mateo because Mateo had helped her when she was a captive of Dr. Bly.

"So, what happened today at Clementine's?" Luke asked.

Morgan filled him in on their visit to Clementine's house earlier, leaving out the part about her morning snooping with Mateo, of course. "What about you? Talk to Dorian Hall yet?"

"I did," Luke said around a bite of garlic bread. "But still nothing yet. No new assignment or anything concerning what happened to Clementine."

"That's odd," Celeste said.

"Yep," Fiona agreed. "It does seem like her death isn't paranormally motivated."

Morgan just nibbled on her lasagna, glad that it

appeared as if they wouldn't have to battle some unknown paranormal enemy. Hopefully this would be a simple case of human malevolence. She needed to steer clear of paranormal altercations at least until she got her gifts back.

"Sorry I'm late." Jake appeared in the kitchen doorway then pulled up a chair beside Fiona at the island. "Got busy doing some research at the office and lost track of the time." He served himself a plate of lasagna and salad then reached for the bread basket. "Found out some interesting information though. Did you guys know there was a professional rivalry happening between Clementine and Rose Degarmo?"

"The fortune teller?" Fiona asked.

"Yep." Jake swallowed a bite of salad. "Seems they got into it a while back, and the police were called."

"When was this?" Celeste asked. "I don't remember it."

"Last year." He leaned an elbow on the table as he chewed, his expression contemplative. "I'm wondering if maybe their rivalry went beyond professional differences and finally boiled over into violence. Wouldn't be the first time one person took out their competition permanently."

"Yikes," Fiona said. "Hard to imagine sweet Clementine getting brutal with anyone. Or Rose Degarmo, for that matter. She's got to be what, sixty?"

"Age shouldn't matter," Johanna said. "Look at what Dr. Bly did."

"True," Morgan said then turned to Jake. "What about your contacts at the sheriff's department? Did you have a chance to talk to them yet about the case?"

"I did, but unfortunately, there wasn't much new information there either. I did find out from the ME though that Clementine died from a blow to the head and that there was a weird mark on her wrist that happened right around the time she died."

"Weird mark?" Luke asked, raising a brow. "Like what? A tattoo?"

Morgan looked at her sisters. When someone died of paranormal means, it left a mark on the body like a burn. Despite what Luke and his agency said, if the killer had been a paranormal, then it was entirely possible they'd killed Clementine by magical means then hit her over the head to try and disguise the real method of murder.

"Not sure. Sheriff White thought maybe it had been caused by handcuffs, but none were found at the scene." Jake finished his first slice of garlic bread then reached for a second. "The ME also said that Clementine was killed in the afternoon, but her body wasn't discovered until the next morning when a client came for an appointment. She lived alone."

Morgan swallowed hard, wondering if a paranormal burn might look like a scrape to the police.

"That's good news," Fiona said. "Morgan was at the shop with me that afternoon."

Jolene screwed up her face. "I thought you said Sheriff White accused Morgan of killing her in the morning?"

"She did," Morgan said.

"Well, technically she said the witness saw your truck there in the morning," Fiona said. "And I wasn't at the shop for a few hours, so you had no alibi. But now you do."

"No, she doesn't," Celeste said. "You were at my hot yoga class from two to four. Remember you took it spur of the moment?"

Fiona's face fell. "That's right. Well, doesn't matter. Morgan doesn't need an alibi because she didn't do anything. We'll be able to prove that rather quickly if the police don't get off their butts and do their job."

Jolene cleared her throat. "What about Rose Degarmo? I've heard of her but don't know her that well."

"I've worked on a few jewelry pieces for her," Fiona said around a mouthful of lasagna. "She's not paranormal as far as I know. Just tells fortunes. Nice lady."

"Hmm." Jolene toyed with the salad on her plate.

"Maybe she's a rogue paranormal. They keep their powers hidden."

"Or maybe Rose doesn't have powers at all, and Clementine's killing wasn't paranormal related," Morgan threw out there.

"Well, that would explain why I didn't sense any paranormal animosity at Clementine's house," Jolene said then frowned. "But what about the mark on her wrist, then?"

"Exactly why we need to continue with our plan, looking at both sides of this case," Celeste said.

Johanna, who'd been quietly eating this whole time, finally spoke up. "I think it's a good idea to explore all the angles."

Morgan took another bite of lasagna, still feeling hopeful that maybe the investigation would lead them to a nonparanormal killer. Rose Degarmo was a good suspect, and hopefully she wasn't a rogue paranormal or at least not one that would put up a fight. Even if she did, Morgan's sisters would be able to subdue her easily even without Morgan's help. Three against one was never good odds. Things were looking up. It made sense too because Jolene had only sensed two energies at Clementine's house, and those could easily have been hers and Mateo's. The logical next step would be a visit to Rose's house to confirm.

"I'm still working on getting a list of the cars like

Morgan's old Toyota," Jolene said, passing the salad bowl around for a second time. "There's a lot of them but not many as beat-up as my sister's. And now we know that Alma's the one who reported it to the sheriff's office. She seemed like quite a character, huh?"

As the others discussed their visit to Clementine's earlier, Morgan's appetite slowly faded under a riptide of guilt. If her gifts didn't recover soon, she'd have to come clean to them. It wouldn't be fair to let them think she was fully operational when she wasn't. Not to mention the extra danger they'd be facing without her intuition to protect them or the fact that she really *had* been at Clementine's and Jolene was off on a wild goose chase trying to prove lots of others had cars like hers.

"We could pay a visit to Rose tonight, if you guys want. I think her shop's open until nine," Fiona said.

"Sounds good to me, but I can't go until after seven," Jolene said. "I still need to stop by Mrs. Tower's place and figure out what's causing all those noises in her shed, and they only happen at a certain time of night."

"How about eight, then?" Celeste suggested. "Jo, you can head there directly from Mrs. Tower's. The rest of us will ride over together from here. That work for everyone?"

Morgan nodded then stared at her plate.

The rest of dinner passed by in a blur of small talk and good company. Fiona, Jake, Celeste, and Cal helped

Johanna clear the table while Morgan walked Luke back toward the front door. He couldn't stay, unfortunately. Said he had to help his brother with something. Jolene had already left for Mrs. Tower's.

Luke leaned in and kissed Morgan again, soft and sweet, then rested his forehead against hers, smiling. "How's your cold? Do you need me to get you any cough drops or Vicks or anything?"

"No. I'm fine. Really."

"Really?" He pulled back to give her a skeptical look. "You didn't eat much at dinner."

"I know. Big lunch earlier." She gave him another quick kiss before hurrying him out the door. "Don't worry about me. I'm good."

Once Luke had left, Morgan rushed up to her bedroom on the second floor. With having to get to Clementine's early in the day, then going back to the shop and having to return to Clementine's with her sisters, she hadn't had any time to try to practice her gifts. Since she had a few hours to pass before they went to Rose's, now would be a good time.

Having that customer return those herbs earlier at the shop had bothered her more than she'd let on. Never, in all her years of herbology, had a client returned a product like that. It was embarrassing. It was humiliating. It was terrifying. And she hadn't missed the look Fiona had given her either at the time, full of an odd mix of curiosity and pity. Thankfully, she'd not brought it up again. But the more lies Morgan told, the riskier things got and the harder it was to keep them all straight.

Belladonna soon scratched and meowed at the door until Morgan let her in. Funny, but if Morgan didn't know better, she'd almost think the cat knew she wanted someone to practice with. She took a seat on her bed with Belladonna in front of her. "Okay, let's practice." She frowned. "But how, exactly?"

"Meow." Belladonna jumped down from the bed.

"Right." Morgan smiled. "You go do something, and I'll try to use my intuition to figure out what you're doing."

She closed her eyes and concentrated since that was what Celeste had done with her spell book the other night and it seemed to work. Focusing hard, an image of Belladonna over by the little fireplace in her room flashed into her mind. Grinning, she opened her eyes, only to find the cat perched on the windowsill instead.

Crap.

She tried again, seeing the cat on the chair this time.

Squinting one eye open, Morgan saw Belladonna now by the door.

Ugh. This wasn't working at all.

The cat batted at a cabinet where Morgan kept a small supply of dried herbs in case of emergency. Maybe she should practice infusing her herbs with power instead. Start small. Good idea.

She pulled out some horsetail and mint then began mixing. Horsetail was a diuretic, so she focused on increasing its potency. That would be pretty harmless, and she could test it out on her sisters without them noticing a thing.

CHAPTER EIGHT

"See? I told you her shop was open tonight," Fiona said as they approached the door of the home where Rose Degarmo lived and operated her fortune-telling business, Forever Fortunes. The home had been built back in the 1920s, and the exterior reflected the Tudor Revival style of that time, with a steep-pitch side-gabled roof, diamond-pane windows, a large semi-hexagon-shaped bay window in the front, and white stucco walls. As they approached the front door, Fiona turned back to Morgan again. "Thanks for the tea, too, by the way. It was delicious. Great aftertaste."

"Thanks." Morgan forced a smile. She appreciated the compliment, but her sister didn't appear to have to use the bathroom any more frequently at all, which was disappointing. And discouraging. She needed to find a focused way to practice that targeted her intuition specifically if she had any hope of getting her powers back. So far, her research had turned up zilch in the way of ideas. Intuition was something most people took for granted, didn't worry about at all. Practicing it wasn't something most people did, so there were few guides or exercises out there to strengthen it. Her doubt demons reared their ugly heads inside her again.

"Let me do the questioning, okay?" Jolene said, knocking. She'd finished her job at Mrs. Tower's just in time to pick them up, and they'd barely had time to chat about their game plan on the way over. "We need answers, but we don't want Rose getting mad and throwing us out."

The door opened to reveal a short, stout Italian woman in her midsixties, with salt-and-pepper hair that stood out around her head in curly disarray. She obviously hadn't been expecting company tonight, if her surprised expression and wrinkled flowered housecoat and slippers were any indication.

"May I help you?" she asked, her tone holding just a hint of Brooklyn. Rose flipped on the porch light then squinted. "Wait a minute. You're the Blackmoore girls, right?"

"We are," Jolene said, flashing a polite smile. "We wondered if we might talk to you for a moment, Ms. Degarmo."

"Oh, well. I suppose." She stepped aside to open the door fully and gestured them inside. "You'll have to excuse the mess. I wasn't planning on having people over this evening and didn't have any clients scheduled. Please, call me Rose."

Morgan took off her coat once they were indoors and handed it to Rose then scanned the living room area where Rose conducted her readings. Pretty much what she'd expected a fortune teller's space to look like. All the furniture was draped in purple velvet slipcovers, with lots of crystal balls scattered about. There were tarot cards, too, strewn over the cushions of a couch and stacked on top of the tables. Decks and decks of them. They seemed somehow familiar, but Morgan couldn't place from where.

"Can I get you ladies something to drink?" Rose walked toward a doorway across the room. Behind her, Morgan could see a bright-yellow-and-white kitchen. "I've just made a fresh pot of tea, or I have coffee too."

"No, no. That's fine, thank you. Our sister Morgan just made us all tea before we left home," Fiona said, earning her a sharp look from Jolene, who probably thought that not accepting the tea was impolite.

They all took a seat in the living room. Morgan perched on the edge of an armchair, eyeing the tarot cards laid out on the coffee table.

Once Rose got settled with her cup of tea, Jolene

dove right into the questioning. "I'm assuming you've heard about what happened to poor Clementine Vega?"

Morgan watched Rose's reactions carefully, concentrating hard to try and get a read on her. Even if her instincts didn't kick in, hopefully it would not be hard to notice the telltale signs of guilt and lying. But Rose didn't look guilty or evasive. The woman exhaled slowly and lowered her head, looking genuinely contrite.

"I have. Such a shame," Rose said. "Clementine and I didn't always get along, and she was quick to bad-mouth me, but I was so sad to hear about her murder. No one deserves that."

She reached over and picked up one of the nearby tarot decks and began fiddling with the cards, flipping them over and laying them out as if doing a reading. The first one she turned up was the seven of swords, and Morgan's heart sank. It was a card that symbolized sneakiness and doing things behind other people's backs.

Rose's gaze flicked up from the deck to lock with Morgan's eyes. Morgan's breath caught at the sense that she'd been found out, all her lies revealed, and that Rose saw right through Morgan's veiled attempts to keep the issues with her powers from her sisters. Perhaps the woman really was a rogue paranormal, like Jolene had suggested.

Panic, hot and strong, surged through Morgan. If Rose said something in front of her sisters and exposed her secrets, it could be catastrophic. She gave a small shake of her head, silently pleading with Rose to keep quiet.

The fortune teller watched her for a moment then gave a curt nod and continued flipping cards.

Morgan exhaled slowly, shoulders slumping with relief.

"Did Clementine's bad-mouthing cause you to lose any business?" Jolene asked, always right to the point. "I can't imagine that it would be good to have a rival spreading rumors behind your back."

Rose snorted, still flipping cards. "Clementine didn't believe in my powers. Thought I was faking it. But she was wrong. I truly do have second sight. It's something you have to nurture though." Her gaze darted to Morgan again before looking away. "Use it or lose it."

So maybe Rose really was a paranormal. But not a rogue. If she were purposely trying to hide her powers, she wouldn't admit to them so freely. Most likely she was one of the many unrecognized paranormals whose powers weren't strong enough to be acknowledged by the community.

"Did you and Clementine argue recently?" Jolene continued.

"No," Rose groused. "I steered clear of that woman. Haven't seen her in months, actually."

"Any idea who might want her dead?" Jolene asked.

"Nope. And before you go thinking it was me, forget it." Rose narrowed her eyes at Jolene. "Why are you asking? Why not the police? Are you looking into the case?"

Jolene managed to look as if she were appealing for help. "Sheriff White wants to blame Morgan, and we figured we'd better do our own investigation."

Rose scowled at the mention of Sheriff White. "Ughh... I don't like that sheriff. Let me see if I can help you out." She set her cards aside and pulled over a crystal ball instead. "I didn't appreciate the rumors Clementine spread about me, but I knew they weren't true. Live and let live, I say. Here, let me take a look in my crystal ball and see if I can find anything that might help shed some light on who might have had a problem with Clementine."

The sisters gathered closer.

"Hmm," Rose said, holding her hands on either side of the crystal ball then closing her eyes. Within the glass sphere, smoke swirled and light glowed. It seemed Rose was telling the truth. She did have the power of second sight. Either that or the crystal ball was rigged somehow. Morgan tilted her head to see if it had an electrical cord. Maybe it ran on batteries. The older woman opened her dark eyes and stared into the crystal ball, frowning. "Huh. Does a white cat mean anything to you girls?"

"Yes! That's Belladonna," Celeste said. "Our pet."

"Good. Good." Rose's hands hovered over the ball, and the light inside it shifted as the scene changed. "Wait, here's something else. A man walking down a remote, wooded street. There's a giant oak to his left..."

Morgan squinted at the image of the person in the ball. His expression looked furtive, as if he were deeply troubled by something.

"Wait! I know him," Fiona said. "That's Benedict Donovan. I just made him an amethyst bracelet last week."

Morgan had been about to ask, but Jolene leaned forward and pointed at the man in the crystal ball. "I know where he's at too! He's on Cross Street, right near Clementine's house, isn't he?"

Interesting. Apparently the crystal ball wasn't rigged, because how else would she have gotten the image of Benedict near Clementine's house?

The sisters peered more closely at the image then exchanged a look. Yep. It was Cross Street all right. Looked like they had suspect number three, and he'd moved right to the top of the list.

"Why would Benedict want a bracelet?" Celeste asked. "Was he seeing Clementine?"

Fiona closed her eyes. "I'm not sure... no, wait. It

wasn't Clementine he was seeing. It was Alma Myers. I remember he told me to keep the bracelet a secret from her."

"That's right. I remember hearing about the two of them." Celeste looked back into the crystal ball. "That explains why he would be on Cross Street. He was going to Alma's, not Clementine's."

"Darn!" Jolene sat back in her chair. "But if he hangs out at Alma's, he might have seen something. The houses aren't that close, but the trees are bare now, and you can see what's going on at Clementine's from Alma's."

"Worth asking him." Morgan was disappointed. Too bad the crystal ball hadn't shown someone clobbering Clementine over the head.

"I guess that doesn't give you any new clues though." Rose sounded disappointed too. She pulled the ball close and rubbed her hands around, trying to conjure up something more helpful. Something red sparked in the globe.

"What was that?" Celeste leaned in.

The center of the globe was mostly white with snow, but partially buried, a navy-and-white-striped knit cap stuck up.

"Looks like a hat," Jolene said. "Could that have something to do with Clementine?"

"It doesn't." Rose waved her hands, and the hat disappeared. "Just a hat in the snow. Meaningless."

While Rose made a few more futile attempts to coerce something useful out of the ball, Morgan's attention drifted to the decks of cards. A jolt of recognition caught her breath. Now she recognized where she'd seen them before. It was the exact same blue and purple colors with stars as the scrap of paper Belladonna had found at Clementine's place the other day.

She looked up at Rose, who was still busy scrying with the crystal ball.

Had the woman been lying about not seeing Clementine for months?

"Sorry, girls, nothing else is coming up." Rose glanced up from the ball, her brows knitting together when her gaze met Morgan's. Probably because Morgan was staring at her a little too intently. Morgan looked away.

"Well, thanks so much for talking to us, Rose," Jolene said, holding out her hand. "You've been very helpful."

"Uh, sure." Rose went to stand.

"Don't get up," Fiona said as they all got up and started toward the door. "We'll show ourselves out. Have a nice evening."

Once back at the curb, Celeste couldn't stop talking about what they'd seen. "That can't be a coincidence. Benedict Donovan on Clementine's street."

"Yes, but don't forget we also learned that Rose really does have paranormal abilities," Fiona added. "And if so, she might have shown Benedict Donovan in there to throw us off track. We did tell her we were investigating the murder. Maybe we shouldn't have tipped our hand."

"And that hat. Do you really think it's meaningless?" Celeste asked. "Maybe she was trying to throw us off track."

"I don't think she was trying to throw us off track. I think Rose was being honest with us." Jolene unlocked the car. "Her aura was purple, not brown like it would've been if she'd been lying. Her second-sight abilities were true, too, as we all saw, but they aren't very strong. I don't think she could have faked what we saw in the crystal ball."

"Still she seemed like she wasn't telling us everything," Fiona said.

"Besides, I found out something else tonight," Jolene said, starting the engine while they all buckled the seat belts. "Mrs. Tower's house is on the river behind Noquitt Beach. The noise in her shed was a skunk, but when I looked across the river, I noticed some paranormal energy."

"Really?" Morgan took that in. In truth, Noquitt Beach was more like a sandbar, with the ocean on one side and the tidal river on the other. If Jolene had noticed paranormal energy, then someone must've been digging there around low tide. Someone paranormal. "Luke didn't say anything about any activity over there."

"Neither did Mateo," Jolene said. "But that doesn't mean someone isn't doing it without the various agencies being aware of it. They have ways to mask themselves."

"Jake didn't mention anything either," Fiona added. That pretty much exhausted their usual channels for intel. "Do you think there's more rogue paras in town? Maybe they had something to do with Clementine's murder."

"Another avenue to check into for sure," Jolene agreed.

"Hey, Fiona. You said you made a bracelet for Benedict," Celeste said. "Do you have his address on file?"

"Probably. I'd have to look when I get into the shop tomorrow." Fiona gripped the back of the front seat as Jolene accelerated away from the curb. "It's too late to pop in on him tonight now anyway. Besides, I don't know him that well. It would be awkward."

As they drove on, Morgan felt more and more restless. First was the whole tarot card thing. Why had a scrap of one been at Clementine's house? Had Rose been there? She wanted to share that with her sisters and get their opinions on it but couldn't because then she'd have to tell them about all the rest. Then there was the fact her tea did not seem to be working on them. Not at all.

So depressing. Giving a last-ditch effort, she blurted out, "Doesn't anyone have to go to the bathroom?"

"No." Fiona gave her a funny look. "Do you?"

"No." Morgan sighed and leaned her head against the car window, defeated.

"Whatever." Fiona gave a dismissive wave. "I have an idea. How about tomorrow I call Benedict and pretend I found some stones that match his bracelet perfectly and ask him if he'd like me to make a set of earrings to go with the bracelet?"

"Do you actually have some?" Jolene asked, glancing at her sister in the rearview mirror.

"I do." Fiona grinned. "It's a great excuse to get him back into the shop, where we can talk to him about why he was on Clementine's street. I mean, who could resist my pretty amethysts?"

"True." Jolene smiled. "Also, we should probably prepare for a paranormal battle, just in case. If nothing turns up with this Benedict guy, we can check out the energy I detected down by the beach."

Morgan's spirits sank further. This was the worst possible time for a battle, at least for her. She'd be no help at all. But Morgan knew talking to Benedict would only be a temporary reprieve. Once her sisters got their minds set on something, it was hard to dissuade them.

She needed to find out more about Clementine's murder and hopefully prove it didn't have anything to do with the paranormal energy Jolene had seen on the beach, and her best lead was the tarot card. Which meant she'd have to find a way to go back to Rose's without her sisters knowing so she could find out exactly what this tarot card connection was about.

CHAPTER NINE

he next morning, Fiona called Benedict Donovan as soon as she and Morgan arrived at Sticks and Stones. He seemed a bit reluctant to come in, but she finally persuaded him to come and look at the stones.

Celeste and Jolene had conveniently dropped by to be there when they talked to the man as well and were busy perusing the new selection of herbs Morgan had gotten in the other day when the bell over the door rang, signaling Benedict's arrival.

He walked in, frowning, looking a bit out of sorts. An unassuming-looking man, Benedict had brown hair and brown eyes, glasses, and a medium build and was maybe in his late fifties. Overall, pretty ordinary.

"Ah, Mr. Donovan. Welcome back to Sticks and

Stones," Fiona said, a bit too loud and cheerful, to let the others know the game was on. "Come over here and let me show you what I think would make a fine pair of earrings for your special someone. Ladies, perhaps you'd like to see them as well."

Morgan, Celeste, and Jolene all made their way over to Fiona's workstation, ohhing and ahhing at the glittery purple gems their sister held up, generally making a show to ensure Benedict would be sufficiently interested.

"Have you met my sisters, Mr. Donovan?" Fiona asked, making the introductions. "Morgan works here as well, running the apothecary. Jolene is an administrative assistant at a local private investigation firm, and Celeste owns the local yoga studio."

"Right, right. Yes, of course. Very nice to meet you all." Benedict smiled at each of them then glanced through the front windows, as if making sure he wasn't being watched. "Uh, please forgive me, ladies, but I must ask you to keep silent about this."

"Really?" Jolene raised a brow at him. "Why? Have you been naughty, Mr. Donovan?"

"No." The guy blushed. "It's just that no one can know I'm here today. The bracelet is a surprise, and I wouldn't want word getting out."

"Of course." Fiona made a lip-zipping gesture. "We are always very discreet here."

"You're dating Alma Myers, aren't you?" Morgan asked.

Benedict gnawed on his bottom lip and blushed. "Why yes. Do you know her? Please don't mention this." He gestured to the stones with shaky hands.

"I might have met her in passing." Not the total truth, but not a lie either. If Benedict knew Alma, then chances were he knew Clementine too. He was acting very jittery, and Morgan had to wonder if it was all just because he was nervous about Alma finding out about the bracelet. Then again, having met the woman, she could see why he might be afraid of her.

Morgan narrowed her gaze on him, searching for any clue he might be hiding something. If only her intuition were working properly, all of this would be so much easier. "What a nice surprise for her, and so generous too. I'm sure she'll appreciate it, especially after all the awful business that happened with her neighbor, Clementine."

Fiona gave Morgan an approving look for her smooth transition into their questioning. "Yes, such a tragedy," Fiona chimed in, her tone appropriately solemn. "Just terrible. Were you at Alma's the day it happened, Mr. Donovan?"

"No, no. Not that day," he said, fidgeting slightly now, plucking at the cuffs of his tweed overcoat. "Both Alma and I were at the church bake sale."

If Morgan's intuition hadn't been on the fritz, she'd have known for certain whether or not he was lying. As it was, she had to judge by the clues instead—his agitation, the way he didn't really meet any of their gazes, how he constantly shuffled his feet. Based on those things, he definitely seemed to be anxious about something.

Belladonna sat in her chair across the room, her icy-blue stare narrowed on Benedict. Morgan got a feeling the cat thought the guy was definitely suspicious. Hope flared anew inside her. Could that be her intuition reawakening? Was it coming back at long last?

Deciding to do a little test to make sure, she excused herself and went back behind her counter to mix a fresh batch of tea. Benedict stayed and chatted with Fiona for a few minutes longer, picking out the settings for the earrings and paying for his purchase. By the time he left, Morgan had a fresh batch of herbs ground and ready to be boiled into tea. Her sisters gathered around her counter to discuss what they'd just learned.

"So, he and Alma *are* an item. Guess that explains why we saw him walking on Clementine's street in Rose's crystal ball," Fiona said. "He must've been going to see his girlfriend."

"Maybe." Jolene was still staring at the door Benedict had just exited through. "But his aura says he might be hiding something."

"Really? You think he could be the killer?" Morgan was hopeful.

Jolene made a face. "Not sure. I didn't read his aura that way. More like he was worried about or keeping something from someone."

"The bracelet probably," Fiona said.

"That doesn't make sense though. If him being there didn't have anything to do with the murder, then why would the crystal ball show it at all?" Celeste asked. "Rose said her powers were strong. Surely she could control her visions then, direct them."

"I'm not sure her powers are all that strong," Jolene said. "If they were, she'd be a full member of the paranormal community and not just an outlier. Not to mention she couldn't conjure up any other clues except a hat. The crystal ball went blank even though she tried."

"Maybe the ball was just showing the general vicinity of the murder, and Benedict happened to be there at the time." Fiona shrugged. "I mean the ball did show Belladonna first, and she was here at the shop with us the entire day that Clementine was killed. Maybe that crystal ball of hers takes time to warm up. Belladonna didn't go anywhere with you after I left the shop that day, did she, Morgan?"

Morgan looked up from her work, eyes wide and throat dry. Not trusting her voice, she just shook her head. She'd concocted her story about being here at the shop that morning. If, in fact, Belladonna had snuck into her car that day when she'd had her appointment with Clementine, then it would need to remain a secret just like all the others.

"Well, I think our next step needs to be verifying that both Benedict and Alma were at the bake sale the day Clementine was killed," Jolene said, thankfully steering the spotlight away from Morgan. "When we're working on a case at the PI office, we work through the clues and information systematically to make sure we don't miss anything. Checking Benedict's alibi would be the next logical step. Did you pick up anything odd from him, Morgan?"

"What? No." She set her tools aside and wiped her hands on the thighs of her jeans. "I mean, it was obvious something was up with him though. He was acting awfully nervous for a man with nothing to hide."

"True." Jolene unwrapped a piece of anise candy from the jar near Morgan's register and popped it into her mouth. "Celeste, don't you know the woman who runs the sale?"

"I do. Harriett Fletcher." She took a piece of candy too. "She started teaching seniors' yoga at my studio." She checked her watch. "Her morning class lets out in a half hour. Why don't we all head there and talk to her?"

"Morgan, you go with them. I'll stay here and tend

the shop," Fiona said, heading back to her workbench and holding up the amethyst stones. "I can't take any more time off now that I have an additional pair of earrings to make."

CHAPTER TEN

They reached Dharma Yoga Studio just as Harriett's class let out. The studio itself was a squat cinder-block building with colorful lotus flowers and Hindu symbols painted on the exterior and a large LED sign out front. The parking lot beside the place was filled with various white-haired ladies in all manner of yoga pants and T-shirts peeking out from beneath their winter coats, some holding their rolled-up mats beneath their arms, all sloshing through the fresh snow that had fallen during the night.

"There she is," Celeste said from the front seat of Jolene's SUV, pointing toward a tall, thin woman with buzz-cut gray hair and a peace symbol emblazoned across the front of her heather-gray top beneath her waist-length bright-pink parka. On the bottom she wore black yoga pants that highlighted her toned legs and the shaggy black fur of her UGG boots. The woman had to be in her late sixties if she was a day, but she looked fit enough to join the Navy SEALs.

Morgan got out of the car and waited for her sisters near the front of the vehicle. The sky above was perfectly blue today, and the wind had died down a bit, making it seem a bit less like the north pole, even if the temperatures were still subzero. Together, she and her sisters approached Harriett Fletcher. She was loading yoga mats and towels into the back of her Subaru.

"Harriett?" Celeste said. "I'm glad we caught you. We were hoping we could talk to you about the church bake sale."

The woman turned to face the three sisters, her skin tanned and her blue eyes sharp with interest. "Anything for you, Celeste. Missed seeing you in the hot yoga classes last week."

"Yes, well, I've been busy." Celeste gestured toward Morgan and Jolene. "These are my sisters."

Once introductions were made, Jolene got down to business. "We were wondering if you remember seeing Alma Myers or Benedict Donovan at the bake sale."

"Oh, sure. Yep. They were there together, in fact. Alma makes the best cinnamon coffee cake around," Harriett said, slamming the trunk of her SUV. "Can't forget something that good. Seriously. It's to die for. I don't go out of my way looking for carbs these days, but that's one food I make an exception for. She sells out every year. Plus, the way she packages them is so cute—all those perfectly matching parcels wrapped in pink cellophane with a tiny bow on top. She's so meticulous about wrapping them, all exactly alike. Makes a great display."

"Wow. Sounds like she goes all out," Morgan said. "Do you happen to remember exactly what time you saw them that day?"

"Oh, gosh. I was so busy trying to keep everything organized and running smoothly." Harriett frowned and pursed her lips. "Sorry, no. The bake sale is always super busy and chaotic. I know I saw them right when the sales started, so that would have been a bit after noon. And she was there when I made a second round about an hour later. Alma had a line at her booth and was trying to handle all those people by herself."

"Where was Benedict?" Celeste asked, frowning. "You said they were there together, right? Didn't he help her run her booth?"

"You'd think he would, huh? That's a good question." Harriett crossed her arms and tapped the toe of her boot against the slush-covered asphalt, her expression thoughtful. "You know, now that I think about it, maybe I did only see Alma that day." She crossed her arms and sighed. "No. That's not true either. Because I distinctly remember the two of them having a tiff. Maybe that's why she was working her booth alone, then. They fought, and he stormed off. I suppose she took off after him a bit later because I noticed her booth was empty. The must have made up because they were together again by the end of the sale."

"A tiff?" Jolene asked. "About what?"

Harriett sighed. "Don't know for sure. I didn't hear them directly, only found out about it later." Then she looked around and leaned closer to Jolene. "But from what others told me, I think Benedict might've had his eye on someone else."

"Really? Who?" Celeste whispered, leaning in closer.

"No idea. He's a bit of an odd duck, if you ask me. Not exactly boyfriend material in my book." Harriett shrugged and pulled her keys out from her pocket to click the automatic starter. The engine roared to life, and the acrid stench of exhaust filled the air. They moved a bit to the side. "But some women like that bookish, nerdy type. Anyway, the scuttlebutt around the yoga studio is that whoever this new woman was who Benedict had taken a shine to didn't return his interest. My opinion? I'd say Benedict should stick to what he's got. Alma's a sure thing." She straightened and narrowed her gaze on the Blackmoore sisters. "Why are you asking anyway?"

"Oh," Celeste said, slinging her arm around Morgan's shoulders. "We were just wondering what kind of baked goods sell best. My sister here is thinking of branching out into herbal muffins at the shop, so we're doing some field research for the shop and heard Alma's stuff was really popular."

Morgan stared at Celeste. She'd come up with that so quickly, and it sounded so natural. Maybe lying ran in the family.

"That's fantastic!" Harriett grinned. "People do love Alma's stuff, but it's all full of sugar and white flour. I've been meaning to talk to Celeste here about adding a holistic snack bar to the yoga studio. Healthy stuff. Juices and protein shakes and bars and the like. Maybe we could do a trial run of selling your baked goods in here too. Bet the ladies would love them."

"That would be great!" Morgan gave Celeste a thanks-a-lot look then plastered on what she hoped was a polite smile as she lied through her teeth. "I'm still in the early planning stages at the moment, but I'll definitely keep that in mind for future development. Speaking of my shop, we, uh, need to get back there before our other sister gets swamped with customers. Thanks again for the information and the invitation."

As she backed away, Jolene rolled her eyes. Celeste appeared to be biting back laughter, and Harriett just looked confused. So much for smooth reconnaissance.

"You could've warned me before you threw me under the bus like that back there," Morgan hissed to Celeste once they'd reached Jolene's vehicle once more. "I had to scramble fast to come up with a lie to get out of it."

Celeste giggled. "You did fine. It was fun to watch. You're a pretty good liar, sis."

Morgan grimaced at that statement but did her best to play it off. Her sisters had no idea how much practice she'd been getting lately.

"Hey, ladies," Jolene said, tossing the keys to Celeste. "Go ahead and get in. I'm going to run inside and use the bathroom before we go. Be right back."

Morgan's spirits lifted as she watched her sister jog back toward the yoga studio. Maybe her herbal tea had finally worked and her gifts were returning at last. She glanced at Celeste, hoping that she, too, would have to use the ladies' room, but she didn't. Darn, maybe her tea hadn't worked, and it was just nature calling. She and Celeste climbed into the car to wait, Celeste in the front passenger seat and Morgan in the back again.

"Looks like Alma and Benedict were both at the bake sale when Clementine got killed." Celeste said after jamming the key into the ignition for Jolene and starting the engine so the car could warm up.

"Yeah. Except Harriett didn't seem certain that Benedict was there the whole time."

"But where would he have gone? And how would he have gotten there? If he came with Alma and they had a fight, they probably took one car." Morgan would have loved nothing more than to pin the murder on something nonparanormal, but she didn't think Alma or Benedict was it. What was the motive? No, her best bet was to find out about the tarot card that was burning a hole in her pocket. If she could only ditch her sisters long enough to go back to visit Rose.

Jolene got into the car a few minutes later, and they headed back toward Sticks and Stones, discussing the case and the new information. "Alma and Benedict were at the bake sale just like they said, so that's one thing off our checklist."

Jolene tilted her head sideways. "Well, Harriett did say she was fuzzy on the timing."

"Yeah," Morgan agreed. "But what motive would they have?"

"I know!" Celeste turned in her seat to look at Morgan. "Harriett said rumor had it that Benedict had his eye on someone else. Maybe the person he had his eye on was Clementine."

"Then why kill her?" Morgan asked.

"Harriett also said the rumor was that the woman did not return his feelings," Jolene said.

Morgan pressed her lips together, trying to picture nerdy Benedict Donovan killing someone because they didn't return his affections. "Really? You think Benedict would kill someone because they turned him down for a date?"

"Yeah, hard to picture that." Jolene tapped her fingers on the steering wheel. "Though that would explain why he was shown in the crystal ball."

"Eh, I'm not so sure Rose's crystal-ball powers are that good." Celeste faced forward again.

"You know, there's one thing we haven't taken into account yet in all this," Jolene said.

"What's that?" Morgan asked, her pulse kicking higher.

"The mark the ME found on Clementine's wrist." Jolene slowed for a red light, and Morgan exhaled slowly. "We didn't get a chance to see it, but it could be from paranormal activity."

"Do you think Jake could get a photo from the cops?" Celeste suggested.

"I doubt they'd just hand that over," Morgan said. "Besides, we don't want Jolene to get into trouble. Given I'm not exactly Sheriff White's favorite person, we should probably avoid the cops as much as possible right now."

"I can ask him anyway. Won't hurt anything," Jolene said. "Thanks for thinking of me though. Besides, Sheriff White hasn't been back to follow up on her accusation since that first day, right? And she hasn't charged you with anything else either. That tells me she doesn't have a leg to stand on. We know you didn't do anything, so I doubt they have any evidence to support her theory. Maybe they even dropped their investigation into you."

"I hope so." Morgan sighed, not believing it for a second. When Sheriff White got her teeth into something, she was like a poodle with a ham roast. "What about your Toyota search? Anything turn up there?"

"Several cars showed up like yours in the area. I'm narrowing it down to see if any of the owners have any paranormal inclinations or knew Clementine or had connections to her business. It takes a while though." Jolene signaled to turn onto the street where the shop was located. "But if Sheriff White isn't accusing you of anything anymore, then maybe I should let that go and focus on the beach energy instead. That could be related."

"We should look at all angles, though I'm not sure it's smart to start something with strangers. Especially paranormal ones." Morgan straightened, clasping her hands in her lap to keep them from shaking. "We've got enough trouble to deal with as it is."

"That's exactly why I think I should switch my research time over from the cars to these other two avenues instead." Jolene parked her SUV in front of Sticks and Stones and cut the engine. "There are only so many hours in the day, and this way I can do a little background checking on possible paranormal suspects before we engage. I mean, we did sense two paranormals at Clementine's even though we didn't sense any bad intent." At Morgan's sharp look, she amended her statement. "Fine. *If* we engage. What's got you so spooked these days, sis?" She met Morgan's gaze in the rearview mirror. "Everything okay?"

"Everything's fine. I'm just being practical." Morgan used the excuse of getting out of the car to avoid eye contact with Jolene. She really was being practical. They had no reason to think that paranormal energy down at the beach was related to Clementine's death, and it didn't make sense to go stirring things up. It didn't help that she couldn't tell her the two paranormals she sensed were herself and Mateo. "Thanks for the ride."

"I'll see you guys later," Jolene, still behind the wheel, yelled out of Celeste's open door. "I've got some work left to do back at the office for Jake on the new PI case we're working. If I've got time, I'm going to check on the tide charts to see when low tide is tonight. I'm thinking it's at six thirty. If so, we should meet up again on the beach and check out the spot where I sensed that energy. See what they were digging for. Meet in the beach parking lot at six?"

Looked like Jolene was going to pursue this no matter what. Morgan didn't dare protest too much. "I don't know. I just got back and—"

Fiona came out of the shop and crossed the porch then walked over to where they were standing near the car, cutting Morgan off. "What's going on? Find out anything interesting from Harriett?"

Jolene relayed what they'd learned and her plans for the meet-up later.

"Sounds good to me," Fiona said. "Things have been beyond slow here at the shop since you guys left, and I got all caught up and even made those earrings for Benedict. Of course, now that we know he has another lady in mind, it makes me wonder who those earrings really are for."

Jolene smirked. "Yeah, no wonder he wanted you to keep it on the down-low. Might not be for Alma."

Fiona nodded. "Anyway, I think we can close up early with no problem at all."

"Well, I'll have to see if I can arrange something," Celeste said. "I'm supposed to teach a yoga class then."

"Hopefully we can all make it. We can investigate that energy and put that theory to bed once and for all. Fiona and Morgan, I'll see you two at six, then," Jolene said. Celeste shut the door, and Jolene drove off.

As the three sisters walked back toward the shop entrance, Fiona watched Morgan carefully. The weight of her stare prickled Morgan's skin, making her already-on-edge nerves even more frazzled.

"What do you say we close up shop now and go get ourselves a pedicure?" Fiona suggested. "My treat."

"Oh, yeah. I'm down for a pedi," Celeste said.

Morgan stopped. A pedicure sounded like heaven, but even better, it would occupy her sisters so that she could go talk to Rose about that scrap of tarot card that Belladonna had found on Clementine's floor. She conjured up a cough and made up another quick fib. "Oh, I'd love to, but if we're closing, I really want to get over to the urgent care about this cold."

Celeste's eyes softened. "Oh, right. Luke mentioned he was worried about that. We'll go with you."

"Oh no! Really. It's so boring there. I'm just going to see if I can get checked out to be sure it's not something serious. Maybe get some cough meds. I wouldn't want you guys to suffer too. Besides, it's full of sick people. No sense in you getting sick too," Morgan said.

Fiona frowned. "Are you sure?"

"Of course," Morgan said, praying her cheeks weren't blazing as hot as they felt. This whole lying thing was snowballing out of control now, and she didn't like it one bit. "I'll meet you guys at the beach."

"Well, okay," Fiona said. "But text us if you need us."

"Of course."

"Okay, then I guess it's just us two." Celeste backed away toward Fiona's Jeep. "You wanna drive?"

"Sure," Fiona said before turning back to Morgan. "Sure you don't want us to go with you?"

"I'm sure." She hated not being honest with her sisters, but until she got this mess straightened out with Rose and got her powers back, she needed to keep them protected.

"Okay, hope you don't have to wait too long." Fiona went back into the shop to lock up, and Morgan got into her truck. She sat there, letting it warm up. As she watched her sisters drive off, she fiddled with the scrap of paper in her coat pocket and wondered when her life had gotten so darned complicated.

CHAPTER ELEVEN

"*A*h. It's you," Rose said half an hour later as Morgan approached her front door again. Talk about seeing into the future. "Figured you'd be back."

Morgan felt flustered. Rose clearly had paranormal abilities, and she knew about the problem with Morgan's gifts. The thing that really threw her, though, was figuring out if the woman was Clementine's true killer and if all this was an elaborate trick. If she was the killer, it might not be very smart to venture inside her house alone, but what choice did she have? She couldn't tell her sisters she'd found a scrap of paper that matched the tarot cards at Clementine's, so she had to check it out for herself.

"Come in," Rose said, gesturing for Morgan to enter and stepping aside to allow her in. "You've got a problem, and I can help."

Morgan stood in the foyer, doing her best not to fidget as Rose took her coat and hat. She slipped the scrap of paper from her coat pocket into her jeans pocket for later. "I'm not sure what you're talking about."

"Stop." Rose held up her hand, shaking her head. "We both know what I saw in that card last night. No sense beating around the bush. Your gifts aren't working, are they? And I suspect your sisters don't have a clue."

Stunned, all Morgan could do was nod. Rose *had* known, and she'd not said a word. Okay. Maybe she should trust this woman after all. She exhaled slowly, willing to at least hear her out. Plus, she could use her problem to get into Rose's good graces then ask her about Clementine's murder, if nothing else. "Yes. It's true. I'm sick about it and have been trying everything I can think of to get them back. I know I need to nurture them and—"

"Calm down," Rose said, holding up her hand. "I've dealt with this before. Let's sit down and discuss a plan of action."

They went back into the purple-draped living room, and Morgan took a seat on the same violet velvet settee she'd perched on before. Rose took the armchair across from her then leaned forward. "First off, do you meditate daily? If not, you should. It's a must these days to keep yourself centered. Next, you need to ground yourself. Carrying lapis lazuli and moonstone usually works well for that." She handed Morgan a small notepad and a pen. "Best write this down so you don't forget."

Morgan did as Rose suggested and jotted down notes.

"I'd also start wearing indigo for the next few days. Make sure you focus on your gifts as much as possible. You can't just expect them to be there. You must *summon* them." Rose's expression was serious. "The universe will manifest what is foremost in your thoughts. If you're walking around stewing about how your gifts aren't working all the time, then that's going to be your reality. It's the secret to everything. Your thoughts become your reality." She sat back and clasped her hands atop her lap, switching directions entirely. "Enough about that mumbo jumbo. Let's get down to why you're really here."

The abrupt shift in topic took Morgan by surprise, and she needed a moment to get her thoughts together. It was now or never. Might as well go for it. Besides, Rose had helped her. Would she do that if she were the killer? No, she'd probably try to get rid of Morgan as fast as she could. Better yet, she would probably have pretended not to be home and never answered the door.

With a deep breath, Morgan fished the small scrap of paper out of her pocket and laid it beside a tarot deck on the coffee table between them. It was an exact match for the pattern on the back of Rose's cards. "I found this at Clementine's house shortly after the murder. You told us before that you hadn't seen Clementine in a long time, but this proves otherwise."

Rose's eyes narrowed. "That doesn't prove anything. I wasn't lying. Lots of clients pass in and out of here each day. Any one of them could've taken a tarot card as a souvenir. Or bought them. I sell the decks along with the crystal balls."

Darn. Morgan hadn't thought of that. Now she realized why there were so many packs of cards and crystal balls. That didn't help narrow things down at all. Anyone could have purchased a deck of tarot cards at any time.

Okay, then while she was here, she might as well ask about Benedict. He'd shown up in Rose's crystal ball last night. Maybe she knew more. "What about Benedict Donovan? He appeared inside the crystal ball. Has he been here? Is he one of your clients?"

"That man from the vision last night?" Rose frowned, her dark brows knitting. "No, he's not one of my *clients*."

Rose's voice was uncertain. Morgan sat forward now, seizing on that new clue. "But he has been here before?"

"Sure." Rose smiled. "I didn't say anything last night, because I don't like to talk about my clients. It's all confidential. But that man was here before with a woman who came in for a reading. She was his girlfriend."

"Alma Myers?" Morgan asked. "Was that her name?"

Rose frowned, concentrating. "Yep. That's the name I remember. She asked me to read her tarot cards and her palm. She didn't have a very stable love line, poor thing." Rose shook her head. "I told her otherwise, of course. Always best for the nonparanormal clients to leave happy."

"What does that mean? How was her love line unstable?"

"Came to an abrupt halt. That's how."

Morgan knew nothing about palmistry. "And that means what? A love line ending abruptly. Trouble between them?"

"Maybe. Hard to say without seeing his love line too."

"And did you?"

"No. He refused. Acted a bit indignant." Rose shrugged. "Some people get that way. But I can't figure a nerdy old guy like that for a killer."

Interesting. Morgan glanced at the crystal ball again, but it was frustratingly blank. So, Alma and Benedict were having issues, at least according to Harriett, and now Rose too. And rumor had it that Benedict had his eye on a new woman. A new idea occurred to Morgan. Had Celeste's guess about that woman being Clementine been correct? That would explain why he'd looked so furtive in Rose's visions. If he was sneaking around behind Alma's back.

Did he really kill her because she'd spurned his advances? But if he was sneaking over to her house to meet with her, didn't that mean he was expected? Maybe even welcome?

Morgan checked her watch. Five forty-five. Time to go if she was going to meet her sisters at the beach. She pushed to her feet and grabbed the scrap of paper from the cushion where she'd laid it and tucked it safely back in her pocket. "Well, thank you so much for your help, Rose. I'll start using these instructions you gave me as soon as I get home."

"Good girl. You do as I say, and you'll be right as rain before you know it. Like I said, I've been through this with many a paranormal client before, and it always works out as it's supposed to in the end," Rose called from her chair in the living room. "Forgive me if I don't see you out, dear. Bad knees, you know."

Morgan raced down to the curb and into her truck, feeling more optimistic than she had since this whole debacle started.

In the dead of winter, the Noquitt Beach parking lot was always empty, so Morgan had no trouble finding a spot. She parked near the long rows of benches that faced the ocean and got out, her mind still whirling with what she'd learned at Rose's.

Brisk salt air stung her face as she walked over to join

her sisters near the edge of the pavement. Jolene had been right. The tide was definitely out, the ocean floor exposed for what seemed like a mile in front of them. The distant crashing of waves still echoed through the fog, adding a haunted feel to the place. The forecasted snow had held off too, and the wind from the day before had left patches of sand visible beneath the previous day's dusting of snow as they walked out onto the beach.

Down a bit was the walkway in the dunes over to the river side. They crossed it, and Morgan was glad to find this area was better shielded and not so cold. Jolene guided them to a spot across from where Mrs. Tower's shed was located on the other side of the river. Here the river wasn't wide—maybe only ten feet across. But miles of sandy riverbank were exposed, and rocks were piled up in various spots. At high tide, the whole stretch would be submerged in water, but since it was low tide, only the thinnest ribbon of river ran through. On the other side were rambling old cottages with large sections of land in between.

Fiona immediately headed for a pile of rocks, putting her hands on them. They glowed slightly beneath her touch. "Something's under here. Not sure what though."

The sound of a car door slamming in the distance had them turning around. Morgan's heart raced, and she searched the area for a place for them to hide in case whoever had been here the night Jolene had sensed the paranormal energy had returned. Moments later, though, Celeste appeared over the walkway to join them. The sisters breathed a sigh of relief.

"I thought you had to teach yoga tonight," Morgan said, swiping a strand of dark hair back under her hood from where it had escaped.

"I did, but I was able to find a substitute instructor to fill in for me." Celeste joined them on the beach. "So I decided to head down here with you guys instead." She'd no more than finished saying that when her eyes got that fuzzy, distant look they always did when she was channeling a spirit from the other side. Without another word to Morgan, Celeste wandered away toward the riverbank, her expression dazed. Morgan glanced over to see Jolene, with her eyes closed, concentrating on the energy fields surrounding the place. Feeling guilty and left out, Morgan closed her eyes too, pretending to use her intuition to sense what was going on here.

It's the secret to everything. Your thoughts become your reality.

Rose's words from earlier swirled in her head. Morgan did her best to picture everything working perfectly in her mind—her intuition strong and true, her instincts on point—but nothing happened. No telltale curl of energy in the pit of her stomach, no shiver of premonition over her skin. Nothing. Her spirits fell once more.

You can't just expect them to be there. You must summon them now.

Tears stung the backs of her eyes. What if she couldn't summon them anymore?

What if her gifts were gone for good?

Finally, Jolene broke the tense silence. "I see paranormal energy starting here and going into the water. They came by boat."

Morgan opened her eyes reluctantly, blinking hard and swallowing around the lump in her throat. Her sisters were all looking at her for confirmation, and she didn't want to disappointment them, so she nodded and said, "Agreed."

"This rock here is a marker. I'd guarantee it." Fiona pointed to the largest of the boulders stacked nearby. "It's really old. Could be a treasure marker."

"Could be," Celeste said, walking back from the river's edge. "I just spoke to the ghost of an old pirate, Captain Brown, who buried some loot here a couple of centuries ago. He says people have been coming for it by boat and digging ever since. But they'll never get through, according to him, because it's buried too deep. The tide always comes back in before they can reach it and fills the holes. In his day, the pirate said, the river didn't rise that high. That's how he managed to bury his treasure here. Just as well, since he said folly will come to anyone who steals it."

"That's great and all, sis, but what does that have to do with Clementine's murder?" Jolene asked.

"Nothing that I can see," Fiona said, snorting. "Maybe Morgan was right, and this murder doesn't have any paranormal involvement."

"I did ask him if the people digging here were Clementine's killers or if they knew anything about the murder, but he said he didn't think so. Said he never heard them talking about murdering anyone. Only getting his riches. He also indicated that they weren't very, er... competent. Though he used more colorful language."

"So, incompetent paranormals?" Jolene stared at the trail of paranormal energy that only she could see.

"But would they be related to Clementine's murder?" Celeste asked.

Jolene shrugged. "Maybe, maybe not. Didn't Alma say something about a bunch of hooligans? Maybe one of them wears a navy-and-white cap."

"I think she only said that hooligans would drive a truck like Morgan's, not that they were at Clementine's," Celeste said.

"Yeah, I guess we still have some investigating to do."

"Well then." Morgan blew on her hands, chilled to the bone despite all her layers. "It's freezing out here. Can we maybe talk about this at home, where it's warm?"

They walked back to their cars slowly, the sound of

the returning ocean doing little to comfort Morgan's sadness. She feared no matter how much practicing and meditating and grounding of herself she did, no matter if she painted her whole body indigo and chanted under the full moon at midnight, her powers might never come back. And if they didn't, then what would she do?

CHAPTER TWELVE

*A*t home, Morgan ran upstairs and changed into an indigo sweater and flannel PJ pants, per Rose's instructions. When she came down to the sitting room, her sisters were all in the sitting room snuggled under soft, fluffy blankets while a cozy fire crackled in the old brick fireplace. She'd also put on her favorite lapis lazuli pendent and had a moonstone stuck in her pocket. Not taking any chances. Nope. The smell of hot chocolate spiced the room along with the soft snores of Belladonna, who was curled up in a plush cat bed just far enough away from the hearth to be safe.

As Morgan entered, the snores stopped, and one ice-blue eye cracked open to stare at her. Darn cat, it was unnerving!

"Hot cocoa?" Johanna lifted the antique Limoges cocoa pot and raised her brows.

Morgan nodded. She was trying hard to stay positive and put good vibes out into the universe about getting her gifts back, as Rose had suggested, and hot cocoa certainly couldn't hurt.

Morgan took her mug and settled into an empty chair.

"I finished my work for the PI case early and was able to narrow down some of the Toyota owners," Jolene said. "To close that out too. None of them were paranormals."

Morgan sipped her cocoa. Good, things were finally going in her favor. Maybe all that positive thinking was working.

"I still say it's too early to rule out that aspect though," Fiona said, remaining dogged as always. Under other circumstances, Morgan appreciated that quality in her sister. It was what had saved her from being falsely charged with murder the last time, after all. But now it only stirred up her anxiety even more. She wished her sisters would just drop that aspect. Fiona continued arguing her case though. "We all know how devious Dr. Bly is, and he could just be lulling us into a false sense of security. Don't forget about the marks on Clementine's wrist. We need to be proactive here. Remember what happened on Rune Island."

"Hmm," Celeste said. "But based on what the pirate's ghost told me, and what Morgan's been saying all along, I'm leaning toward nonparanormal on this one. You know how we always say we have to trust Morgan's intuition."

Morgan choked down a sip of cocoa.

"But if not them, who?" Fiona asked.

"What about Benedict Donovan?" Morgan asked. "He was acting squirrelly earlier at the shop, and honestly, what do we really know about him? After what we found out at the yoga studio, we know that he and Alma were having problems too."

The fact she knew more about the case and couldn't share it with her sisters only made her feel guiltier, but she stuck to facts that they'd all have equal access to. Plus, from what Rose had told her, there was definitely going to be a breakup in Alma's future, but there was no way to share that information that wouldn't result in her sisters wanting to know how she'd found out about it.

But if Clementine had been the "other woman" that Harriett had been talking about, then why would Benedict want to kill her? Maybe he hadn't been responsible for her death though. Maybe he only knew something about it and couldn't tell because it would reveal his interest in her to Alma. And with Clementine dead, he might want to keep stringing Alma along now. That could explain why he'd been acting so strangely at their shop.

"I don't know, Morgan," Fiona said, frowning. "Benedict doesn't strike me as the violent type. I mean, I don't know the guy well, but he's always been very polite and quiet when he's interacted with me."

"It's always the quiet ones," Jolene said.

"True," said Celeste.

Thankfully, before Morgan could say anything more, a knock sounded on the front door. She tossed aside her blanket and padded down the hall, the hardwood floors cold beneath her feet even through her heavy wool socks. Old mansions were beautiful but not exactly great when it came to heating. She put on her best polite smile, which promptly fell when she opened the door and found Sheriff White standing on the front porch.

Apparently she wasn't off the hook with the law just yet.

"Ms. Blackmoore." The sheriff pushed in past Morgan without waiting for an invitation. "I need a pair of your shoes."

"Excuse me?" Morgan asked, blinking. "Why do you need my shoes?"

"Your boots, to be exact," Sheriff White said, her scowl darkening. "I need to compare them to tracks found outside Clementine Vega's house the day of the murder."

"You're kidding, right?" Morgan crossed her arms as her sisters wandered out to join them. "With all the officers tromping around that place, there's no way you can tell any of the footprints found there belonged to the killer."

"Not true," Sheriff White said, giving Morgan a superior look that screamed she wasn't as smart as she thought she was. "A perimeter was established immediately around the premises before any law enforcement entered the area. We photographed and documented all of the snowy areas around the home before we entered the crime scene." Sheriff White's slow smile was chilling. "There was one set we found extremely interesting. A trail of footprints leading to Clementine's back door. Too small to be male. We have reason to believe the killer came in through the kitchen. Adding that to the witness statement putting your car there around the time of death means you are still at the top of my suspect list, Ms. Blackmoore. If you have nothing to hide and want your name cleared, then I suggest you produce a pair of your boots so I can verify whether or not your shoe size is a match."

Morgan reluctantly grabbed the pair she'd been wearing earlier at the beach, which were sitting in the corner by the front door. She handed one to Sheriff White then crossed her arms against the racing of her heart. It felt like it would fly right out of her chest at this point. She'd been put in the local jail for holding once before. She didn't want to go through that again. "What happens if it's a match?"

"Then I take you to the station for further question-ing," Sheriff White said, not looking at her. "You should know the drill by now, Ms. Blackmoore."

The sisters huddled together in a show of solidarity as the sheriff pulled a tape measure out of her pocket and measured the sole of Morgan's boot then pulled out a notepad with a bunch of numbers scribbled in it. The sheriff straightened, scowling. "Your feet are really small. What size shoe do you wear?"

"Six," Morgan said.

"What difference does it make?" Johanna asked, step-ping in between the sheriff and her daughter. "My daughter didn't do anything wrong."

Morgan couldn't help but smile even with the unnerving circumstances. Her mother used to be so frail after what Dr. Bly had done to her, but now she was healthy and fierce and formidable. The fact she was protecting them now warmed Morgan's heart. Seemed the tables had turned.

Sheriff White sighed and shoved her notepad back into her pocket. "Maybe. Maybe not. The footprints weren't the only evidence we found though."

Morgan's throat constricted. Oh boy. Had they found her fingerprints or maybe hair or clothing fibers from her visit to Clementine's? Maybe she could say she'd been there weeks before on some other errand so her sisters wouldn't know she'd been lying to them. Before her panic overtook her, however, her mother stepped in again, bless her heart.

"Did the boots match the prints you found?" Johanna asked, brow raised.

Expression reluctant, Sheriff White shook her head. "No. Too small."

"Then it can't be my daughter," Johanna pointed out.

"She could've disguised her shoe size by wearing someone else's," the sheriff said, her narrow-eyed gaze sweeping across everyone's feet, judging the size of their shoes no doubt. Clearly she was not ready to let this go. "It has been done before. Plus, we have a very reliable witness stating they saw her car there that day. No getting around that. And she was seen earlier tonight disposing of evidence."

"*What?*" all the sisters and their mother said in unison, even Morgan, because she hadn't been getting rid of evidence anywhere.

Sheriff White snorted, placing her hands on her hips. "You all thought you were being sneaky, didn't you? But I've got your ticket. You were down by the beach, and there's only one reason a person would go down there in this kind of weather. To get rid of anything that makes them look guilty. If you helped your sister destroy evidence, that makes all of you accomplices too."

"That's ridiculous!" Johanna said. "My children would never do such a thing!"

133

"You have no idea what we were doing down there," Celeste added. "It's still a free country, isn't it? Maybe we like the ocean at wintertime."

"No one likes the ocean at wintertime." Sheriff White snorted. "Keep talking, ladies. You're just digging the hole deeper."

Morgan wanted to tell the sheriff exactly which hole she could stick her theories into but refrained, given the circumstances. Tensions were running high enough as it was, and Sheriff White had no idea about the paranormals in her community. They couldn't mention the real reason they'd been at the beach, so they needed to bluff their way out of it. More lies. Ugh.

"What evidence?" Fiona stepped forward, matching the sheriff's aggressive stance. "If you're planning on pressing charges against my sister, we have a right to know."

"And we weren't getting rid of anything," Jolene shouted from the back of the group, her tone belligerent. "Like Celeste said, we were just taking a walk. It's nice down there this time of year. Quiet. Last time I checked, communing with nature wasn't against the law, crappy weather or not."

"Not buying it, ladies," Sheriff White said as a cacophony of arguing filled the hallway. "I'm guessing the only thing you were communing with down there was your guilty conscience. Besides, Mary Claybourne saw you all from her house, on the other side of the river. She said you were digging for something."

"Again, not true," Morgan said. "We don't even own a shovel."

She wasn't sure on that point, but it was too late to take it back now.

"Fine. You want to play hardball? I'm game. If you're so set on proving your innocence, then let me inspect the rest of the footwear in your closet for bigger shoes. That will settle this once and for all."

"No." Johanna stayed in front of her daughters, holding firm. "Not without a search warrant. You have one?"

A small muscle ticced in Sheriff White's cheek as she glared at their mother. Silence descended, and the air was thick with tension. Finally, the sheriff ground out, "No."

"Then I'd suggest you come back when you do," Johanna said, opening the door again. "Until then, leave."

Morgan didn't breathe as the sheriff stared at them all for several silent moments.

"I'll be back," Sheriff White said, stomping out into the bitter cold once more. "This isn't over yet."

"Have a wonderful evening," Johanna said, slamming the door, her tone suggesting the exact opposite. "Good riddance."

"This is so insane," Jolene said, putting her arm around Morgan and walking her back toward the warm fire again. "They can't treat you like that. We won't be intimidated."

"No, we won't." Fiona stood on Morgan's other side, an arm around her waist to help support her. "We were on that beach to find out more about the paranormal diggers, not dispose of evidence. No way can Sheriff White prove otherwise."

Celeste and Johanna moved in behind Morgan, effectively surrounding her with love and support. Her chest ached with gratefulness even as her knees wobbled.

They shared a group hug before retreating to their separate blankets and cocoa.

Snuggled in once more, Morgan couldn't resist bringing up the one thing that Sheriff White had mentioned that stuck in her mind. "Evidence must be missing though. Otherwise, why would she have accused us of getting rid of it?"

"Good point," Fiona said. "And I'm guessing whoever killed Clementine had big feet. Or at least bigger than yours, right?"

"Benedict Donovan?" Celeste asked, bless her heart. Morgan hid her smile behind her mug of hot cocoa. "Then again, lots of women wear larger than a size six. It's pretty small."

Morgan's smile faded.

"Do you think Benedict could be in league with Bly's men?" Fiona added. Apparently she was not going to give up on the paranormal theory easily.

Morgan hid her eye roll, barely, and snickers soon broke out amongst the Blackmoore sisters. "He doesn't really seem the type. A bit too human, I'd say."

"True." Jolene chuckled. "But maybe we shouldn't let our guard down about Bly so fast either. He's dangerous, no two ways about it, even if he is half a world away at the moment. Maybe just to be sure, we should go to the seedy side of town to question some paranormals. We can at least find out which ones were out there digging on the beach and make sure the two things really aren't related."

Morgan's heart sank again, and she scrambled to redirect the conversation. She gave a huge yawn and made a show of being tired, which truthfully, she kind of was, especially after Sheriff White's impromptu visit. "How about we sleep on all this and talk again in the morning? It's late, and I, for one, am exhausted."

"Agreed," they all said in unison.

They trundled up to bed after banking the fire and folding the blankets. Belladonna stuck close to Morgan's heels the whole time. Either the cat was trying to give her comfort because she sensed her inner turmoil, or she was just looking for more opportunities to glare at her. Probably the latter.

Morgan knew she needed to do something fast. And she needed her intuition back to do it. Especially if, by some long shot, her sisters were right, and they were headed for a paranormal battle. She'd need all of her skills.

But first, she still needed to do a little more checking on Benedict Donovan.

As she climbed into bed, she concentrated on the positive and took heart from the fact that her tea seemed to have worked better today with Jolene. After all, she'd run to the bathroom after their conversation with Harriett earlier outside the yoga studio, even if nothing had happened with the rest of them. A little bit of progress was still moving forward, right?

Ugh. It was all so confusing.

The universe attracts what you think to you. Don't be negative.

Morgan remained awake, blinking up at the ceiling in the dark with Belladonna curled around her feet atop the duvet. She didn't have time to waste. She had to do something tomorrow before her sisters started poking around on the wrong side of town and got them mixed up in a paranormal war they had no business being in.

Someone could get hurt. And it would all be Morgan's fault.

CHAPTER THIRTEEN

*E*arly the next morning, Morgan dressed all in indigo again—this time a turtleneck and jeans —and put on her lapis pendant and moonstone bracelet before pulling her long black hair into a ponytail. Dressed and ready, she assumed the lotus position in the middle of her bedroom floor and meditated, focusing her mind on the positive. Her tea had worked on Jolene the day before. It was small, but it was a step in the right direction.

Belladonna purred from beside her, and a sudden image of the cat in the kitchen popped into her head. Hard to tell, though, if it was her intuition reawakening or just a need for caffeine.

Half an hour later and meditation completed, Morgan headed downstairs to make coffee. The cat trotted along beside her into the kitchen, stopping near her food bowl. Mystery solved. What she'd seen in her bedroom must have been Belladonna's thoughts. The cat wanted food. Then again, the cat *always* wanted food.

Belladonna stuck close to her ankles as she poured her cat food into a dish and then placed it on the floor. Her sisters wandered in, one by one, each helping themselves to the fresh pot of coffee before gathering around the table. Except for Celeste. She was sticking with her wheatgrass concoction, for clarity, she'd said.

Fiona had a bunch of pebbles in front of her, readying them for battle, if needed. She ran her hands over the pebbles, and they glowed bright red like embers.

"I've been practicing a bit and have been able to infuse emotional energy into the stones." She placed a pink stone on the counter, and it sparked brightly before quickly fizzling out. Fiona frowned. "Okay, I guess that's still a work in progress."

Morgan smiled, but her thoughts were on her own failing gifts. Apparently Fiona practiced things too. Was she the only one who had taken her talents for granted?

Jolene spread out a map of the Noquitt River. "I printed this out at the office. I figure if the paranormals are coming to the river side of the beach by boat, it's got to be close by. Probably not from the ocean side either. It's too cold."

"It's December," Morgan said after she'd fixed her

own mug of liquid energy and taken a seat at the bar across from Jolene. "Most of the hotels are closed, so I think any strangers putting a boat in the water from one of their lots would be way too conspicuous. It must be one of the cottages farther down."

"That's what I was thinking too." Jolene traced the length of the river with her finger. It was dotted with small cottages along a mile stretch before the river got too thin to be of interest. "Some of these cottages are rented out for the winter. I want to do a drive-by later and see if there are any old red Toyota trucks like yours."

Morgan's stomach swooped. Darn! Jolene was still trying to find that truck. Well, she wouldn't find it at any of the cottages. At least Morgan doubted she would. Maybe that was a good thing. If she didn't spot the truck, then maybe that would slow down the altercation with the paranormals that it seemed her sister was not going to give up on. Maybe it would buy her some time to find the killer and avoid the conflict all together.

"I'll go with you," Celeste said. "The sooner we confront these guys, the sooner Sheriff White can back off."

"Yeah, I don't like the way she came for your shoes, Morgan," Fiona said. "She must still have you on the suspect list."

Morgan couldn't shake the storm cloud of anxiety building inside her. She needed to hurry up and figure out if Benedict Donovan was Clementine's killer before her sisters plunged them into a deadly paranormal confrontation or Sheriff White arrested her.

Across the room, Belladonna finished her breakfast then hopped up on the sill of one of the large windows. Morgan glanced outside to see a crimson cardinal perched in the big oak tree, bright and colorful against the snow that had fallen overnight.

The color reminded her of Alma's red ranch house down the way from Clementine's, which then led her to think of Alma, which led her to—

Wait a minute...

Perhaps she'd been approaching this all wrong. If Benedict was the killer, he sure as heck wouldn't come out and tell them. But there was one person who might know something. The person who was closest to him. Alma.

She could go see Alma this morning on her way to the shop. She'd use picking up coffee as an excuse.

Benedict had said he was at the bake sale at the time of the murder, but Harriett Fletcher had also said he stormed off after he and Alma had argued. She'd assumed he'd been in the building, but what if he hadn't? What if he'd left to kill Clementine? Perhaps Alma would be able to shed more light on the situation and help prove Benedict's guilt... or innocence.

CHAPTER FOURTEEN

ust before eight a.m., Morgan hurried through the snow on Cross Street again, past the big oak tree they'd seen that night in the crystal ball at Rose's. In the vision, the tree had been on Benedict's left though, meaning he hadn't been going to Alma's. He must've been heading for Clementine's. Bingo! She was on the right track.

She'd parked down the street because she knew Alma was the one who had told Sheriff White about her car. She didn't want Alma to recognize it. That might complicate things. But she also didn't have long. She'd told Fiona she was stopping for gas and then picking up coffee and was expected at the shop. She couldn't delay.

Morgan could see a light on and someone moving around inside Alma's house. Good, the woman was up. Morgan headed up to Alma's door and knocked. The curtain on the side panel fluttered, then Morgan heard the deadbolt click, the chain slide, and finally the door opened, and Alma gave her a dark, suspicious look.

"Can I help you?" the older woman asked. Today she was dressed in gray slacks and a white sweater, her short white hair a bit mussed as if she'd just gotten up not too long ago. As she recognized Morgan, her brown eyes narrowed even further. "Aren't you one of the Blackmoore girls who was snooping around Clementine's the other day?"

"I'm sorry to come by unannounced," Morgan said, hoping to get into Alma's good graces. "I was hoping to talk to you a bit more about Clementine."

"Clementine? Well, I don't know much about her, like I already told you." Alma's eyes widened. "Oh dear! Has someone else been killed? I told you it's not safe out."

"No one's been killed," Morgan assured her and forced a polite smile. "I just have a few questions."

After a moment, Alma stepped aside. "Well, hurry up then. You're letting all the heat out." She waved Morgan inside then shut the door behind her and slid the deadbolt and chain into place.

The interior of the house was quaint and charming, a sort of hodgepodge of antiques and knickknacks collected over the years. A cheery fire blazed in the fireplace, and the air smelled of cinnamon and baking bread.

"I was just getting ready for breakfast. Can I get you some tea?" Alma asked, walking into the kitchen and leaving Morgan standing alone in the living room. The older woman kept wringing her hands, as if she were flustered. Or nervous. "I do hope the killer isn't still in the neighborhood. You know an old woman like myself isn't safe alone."

"He won't be back. But it might help to catch him if you answer a few questions." Morgan pulled off her knit hat and tucked it into her pocket, then took a seat on a Victorian-style settee, the static in her hair crackling around her head. She unbuttoned her coat but didn't take it off. The temperatures last night had dropped to subzero again. It would take a while for her to thaw.

"What kinds of questions?" Alma asked from in the kitchen.

"Oh, the usual stuff. Who you saw. If you saw anything unusual over at Clementine's that week."

Alma's reply was tinged with mistrust. "And why would *you* be doing that? You're not with the police."

"I'm just trying to piece together a timeline on the day Clementine died. If there was something unusual going on, it might lead to the killer."

"Unusual?" Alma leaned out of the kitchen to frown

at Morgan. "I told the police about the red truck and those ruffians with their pom-pom hats."

"Ruffians with hats?"

"Yes, there was a gang of them who came to visit her the other day. All bundled in ski gear and striped knit hats. Didn't I tell you that before?"

"No." The image of the striped hat they'd seen in Rose's crystal ball came to mind. Could that really have meant something? But if the ruffians were the killers, then what about Benedict? What if those ruffians were the paranormal treasure hunters Jolene had sensed digging at the beach? That was the *last* thing Morgan wanted. No, it was too far-fetched. The killer *had* to be nonparanormal. It had to be Benedict.

"Are you daft? I seem to recall mentioning that beat-up truck to you and your sisters. Anyway, I told the police. Those boys were angry when they left. They weren't in the truck that day, but if you ask me, it's them who did it. Probably came back to finish her off later on." Alma emerged with a tray filled with a teapot, two cups, and a plate of buttery, toasted cinnamon-swirl bread. She set it all on the table then poured tea for each of them before taking a seat in a Queen Anne–style chair across from Morgan, fiddling with the amethyst bracelet on her wrist.

The amethyst bracelet Fiona had made for Benedict?

Morgan tilted her head for a better look. The bracelet

hung large on Alma's wrist, and she tucked it over her sleeve for a better fit. There was no mistaking the craftsmanship. It was the bracelet Fiona had made. So Benedict had given it to Alma after all. Did that mean they'd made up? Maybe now that Clementine was out of the way, Benedict was making an extra effort to appease Alma.

"Did you see them the day she died?" Morgan asked. This wasn't really going in the direction Morgan had hoped. Who were these "ruffians"? Was it another lead she should follow?

"How should I know? They were here. Now she's dead." Alma nibbled a piece of toast and fiddled with the bracelet again.

Darn. Morgan would have to look into who these people were and why they'd left angry. How could she figure that out? She still needed to find out more about Benedict and if he really was at the bake sale all day. That image of him in Rose's crystal ball *had* to mean something, and it was a much more solid lead than some "ruffians" who she'd probably never be able to track down.

Alma's bracelet jangled again. Perfect, she could use the bracelet as an excuse to bring up Benedict. Morgan nodded at the bracelet. "That's a lovely bracelet. My sister Fiona made it."

Alma tucked the bracelet protectively under her sleeve. "It was a gift from Bennie."

"Benedict Donovan, right? Such a thoughtful man."

Alma straightened in her chair. It seemed like she was uneasy. Was that because she and Benedict were having some trouble? Or maybe she suspected this relationship with Clementine all along. "He is very thoughtful."

"Um, I wondered if things were okay between you and Benedict."

"I don't really see that it's any of your business. You young folks need to learn how to be more polite."

Morgan blushed. She supposed she *was* being rude. Her mother would be disappointed in her, but she was desperate to know whether or not Benedict really had an alibi. "Sorry. It's just that he seemed so excited when he ordered that bracelet, but then Harriett Fletcher mentioned something about a big argument between the two of you at the bake sale."

"Well, that busybody. I don't see that it's any of her beeswax." Alma leaned forward. "What did she say?"

Morgan glanced out the window, wondering if she should tell Alma about the rumor of Benedict and another woman. Should she mention they thought it might be Clementine? The only suspicion of that was the image in Rose's crystal ball, and she doubted Alma would put stock in that. Though Alma had gone to see Rose herself. Probably best to be vague.

Morgan felt bad spreading rumors, but if Benedict really was the killer, she would be doing Alma a favor. If she planted a seed of doubt, at least she could get Alma thinking about some of the discrepancies in Benedict's story. Alma might be able to provide her with the proof she needed, and Morgan could possibly even be saving Alma from becoming his next victim.

Morgan took a deep breath. "She said something about a fight between you and Benedict over another woman."

"Poppycock!" Alma straightened in her chair. "Bennie loves me."

But her voice had an undertone of doubt. Something was up between the two of them, but Alma just didn't want to admit it to herself. Morgan had to make her see the light. "Harriett said that Benedict stormed off and you both were gone for a while. Did you have a fight and make up?"

Alma looked down and fiddled with her teacup. Morgan remained silent. She could tell Alma was wrestling with her own emotions, as if she suspected something but didn't want to believe her own thoughts. Wait. Was she getting her intuition back, or was she so desperate for Benedict to be the killer that she was seeing things that weren't there?

"We did have a fight." Alma fidgeted with the bracelet. "And Benedict did storm off. Unusual for him, he's usually such an even-tempered man. Anyway, it was very disturbing to me, and I had to take some time to pull myself together."

"That's understandable. And did you make up with him?"

"Not until later that night." Alma glanced out the window. "I was in the ladies' room for a long time and never saw him until it was time to leave."

Bingo! Benedict wasn't with Alma that afternoon when Clementine was killed. Which meant he likely had no alibi. Now if she could only figure out how to prove he'd come back here and killed Clementine.

"Did you say you left together?" Morgan asked.

Alma nodded. "We drove to the sale together and only had one car, so naturally we had to leave together. Luckily we made up before that."

"Did you go anywhere in the car in between? Or did Benedict?"

Alma looked confused. "I don't think so. Why do you ask?"

"Oh, no reason," Morgan said. "And you didn't see anyone suspicious over at Clementine's that night when you got home."

"No. The windows were dark, and I just assumed

she'd gone out." Alma shuddered. "I had no idea she was laying in there already dead."

"It's scary, isn't it? But if you can think of something —anything that you saw—it might help capture the killer." Morgan got up to leave. She'd planted the seed, and she'd have to hope that it would grow and Alma would come up with something she could use against Benedict. It must have been working, because as she walked her to the door, Alma grabbed a pen and paper from a little table.

"Let me get your number, and I'll call or text you if I think of anything else."

Morgan gave her cell phone number and left with a smile. Alma knew something about Benedict. Morgan was sure of it. Alma only needed some time to convince herself to tell someone else. Hopefully that someone else would be Morgan. And hopefully that would happen before her sisters got them into a paranormal fight they might not win.

CHAPTER FIFTEEN

*M*organ was lucky she didn't get a speeding ticket on her way from Alma's to the coffee shop and then to Sticks and Stones.

She hurried into the old cottage, a swirl of snow following her inside the door before she pushed it shut with her hip, seeing as she had a steaming white Styrofoam cup in each mittened hand.

"Long line at the coffee shop this morning," Morgan said by way of explanation for her lateness.

"Uh huh." Apparently Fiona had been immersed in her task of making a citrine pendant and seemed oblivious to the fact that it had taken Morgan an extra-long time to gas up and get their coffees. She never even looked up as she used one of her tools to form a metal frame for the stone.

Belladonna was another story. She didn't move from

her position curled up in the chair but managed to slit open one eye to give Morgan a judgmental look, as if she knew where Morgan had *really* been.

Fiona set the pendant aside and lifted an amethyst earring, which had been sitting on her worktable, up to the light. It glowed purple where the sun filtered through the partially translucent gemstone.

"Not bad, huh?" Fiona asked as Morgan handed her the coffee.

"Those go with the bracelet Benedict had made for Alma?" Morgan flipped up the plastic tab of her Styrofoam cup and sipped her yerba mate tea. Unlike Fiona, who was drinking a latte and needed gallons of caffeine to keep fueled, Morgan preferred hers at a slower pace.

Fiona nodded. "He's getting a bit tedious though. Gave me a stern warning not to tell Alma again when I called to tell him the earrings were ready."

Morgan frowned. That was odd. "When did you call him? Yesterday?" Maybe Benedict had given her the bracelet this morning.

Fiona placed the earring and its mate gently in a velvet-lined case and shrugged. "Nope, just before you came in. He is kind of an odd one."

That made more sense. Fiona had called about the earrings, so Benedict probably meant not to tell Alma he had matching earrings for the bracelet. Probably saving them for a gift of some sort. Either that or maybe Benedict was up to something else, but what? Was this something about hiding the fact that he was Clementine's killer?

Fiona glanced up at Morgan. "Do you really think Benedict could be the killer?"

"Well, he is acting strange. And Harriett said he wasn't at the bake sale the whole time, and—" Morgan bit off the words. She couldn't tell Fiona that Alma had said she didn't see him after the fight.

"Well, what does your intuition tell you?" Fiona persisted.

Morgan turned away on the pretext of going back behind her counter. But the real truth was she was afraid Fiona read the truth on her face. The truth that her intuition was telling her bubkes.

"My intuition says he's guilty of something," Morgan said.

"Meow!"

Belladonna stirred in the chair, stretching her paws far out in front of her and humping her back, all the while staring at Morgan with those judgmental ice-blue eyes.

Morgan spun around and got busy mixing up some herbal remedies. Thankfully most of her requests this time of year included herbs like eucalyptus and chamomile for coughs and colds. Those would always work, no matter how dull her magic had become.

As she worked, she glanced at her phone sitting on the counter. Maybe Alma would call or text. She was certain Alma had asked for her number because she was on the brink of something. If Alma didn't contact her soon, Morgan would have to figure out a way to trap Benedict into admitting he was the killer or get some concrete evidence against him.

The bells over the door tinkled as Jolene and Celeste swept in, stomping snow from their boots onto the mat in front of the door before tossing their coats onto one of several hooks hanging on the wall.

Belladonna trotted over to wind around Celeste's ankles, and Celeste bent down to pet her.

"Well, that was a bust." Jolene picked a mint out of the glass apothecary jar on the counter near the old-fashioned nickel-plated cash register, tore off the end of the wrapper, and slid it into her mouth.

"No red Toyota?" Fiona asked.

For a moment, Morgan was confused, and then she remembered that Jolene and Celeste had gone on a recon mission to see if there were any red Toyotas parked at any of the cottages on the river. She'd forgotten about it because she knew the red Toyota Alma had seen was actually hers. Hopefully Alma hadn't seen her driving away in it today, though she thought she'd seen the curtain flutter in the window as if Alma'd been watching. Morgan hoped she'd parked far enough away that Alma wouldn't realize it was her pulling away in the truck. She supposed it didn't really matter what Alma thought. Sheriff White already thought it was Morgan's truck that had been there.

"I suppose they could be out driving somewhere in the truck," Fiona said.

"Or our treasure-digging paranormals are not staying in those cottages," Celeste said.

"Or they're not the killer," Morgan added.

Ding!

Too bad it wasn't Morgan's phone. It was Jolene's, and she dug it out of her pocket and looked at the display, then her face split into a smile. "Things are looking up. It's a message from Jake. He managed to get a picture of the crime scene from the police."

They all gathered around. Pictured on her phone was Clementine's kitchen. Clementine's body lay on the floor, the chair tipped over just like Morgan had seen it except the body hadn't been there when Morgan investigated.

"Looks pretty similar to what we saw," Fiona said.

"Still seems like she knew her killer. It looks like maybe they were even sitting at the table," Celeste added. "Whoever she was drinking with might have made an excuse to get up for something and then clobbered her from behind."

"I don't think they were necessarily sitting at the table. If they were paranormals, they could've lulled her into a false sense of his security or messed around with her energy. Maybe she went into the kitchen to get the tea and had to sit down in the chair because they drained her energy, then they came in and hit her in the head." Fiona tilted her head to get a better look at the photo on Jolene's phone. "Or maybe she wasn't even sitting in the chair. She could have been standing, preparing the tea, when they snuck in and clonked her on the back of the head or zapped her with paranormal energy. Maybe when she fell, she grabbed onto the chair and took it down with her."

"Yeah, could be. Let's see if we can get a better look at the mark on her wrist." Jolene used her thumb and forefinger to zoom in on Clementine's wrist. "Well, it's a little grainy, but that doesn't look much like a burn to me. More like a rug burn."

Celeste took the phone for a closer look. "And it's sharp like a cut. Not like paranormal energy."

Fiona stood back and crossed her arms over her chest. "You know, maybe this doesn't have to do with paranormals." She glanced at Morgan. "You've been thinking all along it's Benedict. When are we ever going to learn to trust your intuition?"

Morgan produced a wry smile. Yeah, now probably would not really be the time. But she couldn't say that, so she kept silent.

"I think you guys are right, but... hey!" Jolene

snatched the phone and moved her fingers over the display, zooming out and then in again but on a different area. "Check this out. Look at this hat."

They all bent over to look at the phone again.

"It's a navy-and-white-striped hat." Fiona stepped back and looked at them.

Morgan stared at the phone. She didn't remember seeing a hat when she'd gone to Clementine's alone, but she supposed she might not have noticed because they hadn't seen the hat in Rose's crystal ball yet. Or maybe the police had taken it as evidence?

"That's just like the one in Rose's crystal ball," Fiona said.

"But it's not lying in the snow like we saw in the crystal ball, and Rose said the hat had nothing to do with Clementine's murder," Morgan said.

Jolene pursed her lips. "I thought she acted a little cagey about that."

Celeste nodded. "Besides, that's what she *said*, but what if she was lying? What if Rose knows more about this than she let on?"

Fiona grabbed her coat off the hook. "Then I say we need to make another visit to Rose Degarmo to find out *exactly* what she does know."

CHAPTER SIXTEEN

*R*ose didn't look happy when she opened the door. "You girls again?"

Jolene brushed past her into the house. "Yeah, it's us again. Maybe if we'd gotten what we came for the first time, we wouldn't be back."

Rose shut the door and crossed her arms over her chest. "What's that supposed to mean?"

Jolene turned to face her. "I think you know."

Rose's gaze scanned the girls, lingering for a few beats longer on Morgan. Morgan's gut clenched. Would Rose tell her sisters that she'd come back once before? Morgan had tried to dissuade them from coming, partly because she didn't want any chance of Rose spilling her secret but also because she didn't really think Rose had anything to do with Clementine's murder. Rose had proven she was trustworthy. She'd tried to help Morgan with her problem. She wasn't some nefarious killer or accomplice trying to hide things from them. Was she? But since she couldn't tell her sisters too much about the reason she felt Rose was trustworthy, her efforts had been in vain.

Morgan held her breath, waiting for Rose to tell her sisters about her solo visit, but she didn't. She simply shook her head and started toward the purple velvet room with the crystal balls and tarot cards. The smell of incense hung in the air. "Come on in, I suppose. I'm actually not surprised to see you. I figured you girls would be back. I know you haven't figured out who killed Clementine yet."

"Right. And that's no thanks to you," Fiona said.

"What do you mean? I don't know anything about Clementine's death. I told you that before." She gestured toward the crystal ball sitting on the table, and it glowed pink for a second. "I did my best to show you what came up in the crystal ball."

Jolene's eyes narrowed. "Not everything."

Rose looked genuinely confused. "What are you talking about? I showed you everything."

"Maybe you showed us everything, but you might've tried to mislead us. In fact, maybe that was on purpose," Celeste said. "You and Clementine were rivals, and I heard there was bad blood between you."

Rose rolled her eyes. "We've been over this. Yes, she

said some stuff about me. Didn't believe in my abilities. She wasn't the first and won't be the last. But if I killed everyone who talked trash about me, there'd be a trail of bodies." Then she frowned. "What do you mean I held stuff back?"

Fiona gestured toward the crystal ball. "The blue hat. We saw it in there, but you said it had nothing to do with Clementine's death."

"You mean the navy-and-white-striped one that we saw in the snow?" Rose went over to the crystal ball and ran her hands over the top. The image of the hat came up.

"Yes, that hat." Celeste pointed at it.

Rose laughed. "That's got nothing to do with Clementine. That's got to do with me. That hat belongs to a dumb paranormal kid who came by wanting information." She huffed. "Stupid kids these days think they can get something for nothing. Think everything is owed to them. Think it's easy to dig up a centuries-old treasure."

Jolene and Celeste exchanged a glance. Morgan's gut clenched even tighter. The hat belonged to the paranormals who were digging up the treasure? Could this get any worse? Morgan glanced at the crystal ball again, wishing for another image of Benedict, preferably one of him hitting Clementine over the head in her kitchen. But the ball had gone dark.

"You mean paranormals came here about a treasure?" Fiona asked.

Rose nodded. "Yeah. They're not the brightest stars in the universe either. Wanted me to conjure up the location of some old treasure down at the beach."

"And did you?" Celeste asked.

Rose snorted. "You think I'm stupid? First of all, my gifts don't work that way. I can't just conjure up the location of a treasure, and second of all, I've talked to Captain Brown's ghost. He's nasty, and I don't want him haunting me because I gave up the location of his treasure. Not that I know where it is."

"So, what happened when they came here?" Jolene asked.

Rose gestured toward the crystal ball. "It started off nice and friendly. They pretended they wanted readings. But they didn't fool me. I sensed they had something on their minds. When I finally got it out of them, they demanded I show them where the treasure was."

"But you didn't?"

"Nope. Like I said, I don't know where it is and don't want to know. They got pretty mad about it. Made some idle threats, especially that one with the stupid striped hat. I wanted to yank that thing off his head, but I ended up getting out my broomstick and chasing them off."

"They ran away afraid of a broomstick?"

Rose nodded. "Yep. Told you they weren't too bright.

Course I might've put a few sparks on the stick and told them it was going to magically castrate them."

Morgan's sisters glanced at each other. She wasn't sure if they believed Rose's story. Did she want them to? Why would Rose lie about the hat? She'd have no reason, but this didn't bode well for her. The last thing she wanted was for her sisters to go off on a hunt for these paranormals, even if they weren't very bright.

"And then what did they do?" Fiona asked.

"How would I know? Maybe ran home to their mommies. Their paranormal powers were amateur at best. I guess they must not practice them often enough." Rose slid her eyes over to Morgan, and Morgan's heart leapt into her throat.

Celeste put her hands on her hips and gazed down at the crystal ball. "I bet they went to Clementine after they came here. That's why the hat was in the crystal ball."

Rose made a face. "Why would they go there? Clementine is a healer not a visionary. Besides, the ball showed the hat in the snow. Could be anywhere."

"Yeah, but if they are as stupid as you say, they probably don't know the difference," Celeste said.

Rose's brows shot up. "Huh, you have a point." She glanced at the crystal ball. "Maybe that vision did have something to do with Clementine."

"And if they were getting desperate to find that treasure, maybe they got a little angrier at Clementine's than they did here," Jolene added.

"But there was no sign of a struggle at Clementine's," Morgan said. That seemed to indicate it wasn't angry paranormals, didn't it?

"True. Maybe they picked up after or something. But it's worth checking out. Because if they were getting desperate and they went to Clementine's and Clementine didn't tell them where the treasure was, well then..." Jolene held her hands up and shrugged. "Maybe they got angry enough to knock her over the head and kill her."

"But the hat wasn't found in the snow. It was in her kitchen," Morgan pointed out.

Rose glanced at the crystal ball then back at Morgan. "In her kitchen?"

Jolene nodded. "We saw it in a photo of the crime scene. Why would the crystal ball show it in the snow?"

Rose shook her head. "No idea on that one. But if you say it was in her kitchen, then I guess that proves those boys were in her house."

Jolene glanced around at her sisters. Morgan didn't like the glint in her eye indicating that Jolene's next step would be to confront these paranormals and see if they had killed Clementine.

"Okay. Thanks for seeing us." Jolene nodded at Rose and headed toward the door with the rest of them following.

Morgan took up the rear, shooting Rose a slight nod of thanks on her way out. Rose hadn't told on her to her sisters, and for that she was grateful. She made a mental note to make an herbal concoction for Rose as a gift later on. When she joined her sisters on the street, they were excited, and Morgan's spirits fell even more.

"We need to find these paranormals now and question them." Fiona whipped open the passenger door of Jolene's SUV and jumped in.

"I agree." Jolene jumped in the driver's seat. "But let's not be hasty. First we need to get home and assemble some things just in case a fight breaks out."

"You think we can trust her?" Celeste looked back at Rose's house from where she'd slid into the back seat next to Morgan.

"Probably." Fiona turned to look at Morgan. "What do you think?"

"Yep, I think we can definitely trust her," Morgan said. At least she knew she could trust Rose to keep her secret about her intuition. About other things, she wasn't so sure, but she was too busy trying to think of a way to get her sisters to delay the confrontation to think more about it. If only Alma would come through with something concrete.

"Good." Jolene pulled away from the curb. "Now if we can figure out where those paranormals are staying, it probably won't be hard to get the truth out of them."

"Especially if they are rank amateurs like Rose implied," Celeste added.

"Should be easy peasy with our combined skills." Jolene thrust her fist out, and the four of them did a four-way fist bump while Morgan tried to hide her feelings of trepidation behind a wide smile that she prayed didn't look as fake as it felt.

$\mathcal{B}$y the time the sisters got home, Johanna was just taking a pot roast out of the oven. They filled her in while they helped her with the rest of the meal and put out place settings at the breakfast bar.

"We better get a move on," Jolene said once the last of the dishes were in the dishwasher. "I want to get a confession out of these guys before Sheriff White finds more trumped-up evidence against Morgan."

"Don't forget to use your new stones," Johanna called after Fiona as she rushed from the room.

Morgan watched her mother absently while she desperately tried to figure out how to delay her sisters. For a woman who had once been held captive by an evil paranormal, Johanna was acting awfully calm, sitting at the breakfast bar, dunking a teabag into a mug of steaming water.

Johanna caught her look and smiled. "I don't think you girls have anything to worry about. If these paranormals aren't particularly skilled, as Rose suggested, then it should be easy. You girls have really been honing and practicing your skills. You're all so much stronger than even a year ago. I don't think too many could defeat you."

Morgan cringed inwardly. Honing and practicing? Maybe her sisters had been, but her loss of her gifts seemed to indicate that *she* hadn't been doing it nearly as much as she should have.

Maybe she should try to get a meditation session in before her sisters insisted she head off to battle. Come to think of it, that would serve two purposes. It might help her intuition come back, and it would also delay them. Hopefully long enough for Alma to remember something suspicious about Benedict. Because more and more now, Morgan had the feeling that the killer was not the paranormals but someone very human. And very deadly.

Jolene and Celeste were in the front parlor. The room, which was not often used, was furnished with Blackmoore family antiques including carved rosewood furniture and brass and glass lighting and completed with drippy crystals, stained-glass windows, and gilt-framed paintings of long-dead ancestors. It had a certain old-world ambiance, and Jolene claimed the energy in the room always helped her replenish her gifts.

Jolene was standing in the middle of the room, shoving a blue drusy geode into a big tote bag.

"This is azurite. It has truthfulness energy. We might be able to aim it at the paranormals and get the truth out of them," Jolene said.

Geodes were known for exuding high energy. Morgan knew from experience that one had to be careful when facing the open end that had all the crystals. She unconsciously clutched at the amulet around her neck. Fiona had fashioned them for her sisters from obsidian because that helped intercept the energy and bounce it back at the perpetrator. Hopefully Morgan wouldn't end up in front of the geode herself, or she'd have to make quick use of the amulet before she ended up spilling the truth about her lack of gifts to her sisters.

"And I'm going to use some azurite to cast a truthfulness spell on them." Celeste tossed a few blue rocks into the air and caught them. "Speaking of which, I better get to the library. I need to meditate to clear my head so that I'm at the top of my game tonight."

"Good idea," Morgan said. "I need a refresher meditation too. And besides, my intuition tells me we don't want to confront them until later, when the moon is out."

Jolene stopped what she was doing and looked at Morgan. "Oh really? Okay, then that's what we should do. We're always saying we need to trust your intuition more. We'll wait until later tonight."

Wracked with guilt over the lie about her intuition, Morgan climbed the stairs to her room. She really was going to meditate, but her main reason was to delay the confrontation with the paranormals.

She wanted to buy time for Alma. She was hoping that if she stalled long enough, Alma would contact her with some proof about Benedict. If Benedict was the killer, there was no sense in getting into a fight with these paranormals. Even though by all accounts it seemed like her sisters could whip their butts without her, a confrontation might reveal to them that she was no longer in control of her gifts.

While it appeared that her mother and her sisters were oblivious to the fact that her intuition had failed her, Belladonna, with her knowing looks and judgmental meows, wasn't quite so oblivious. Much to Morgan's dismay, the cat followed her up and would not be dissuaded from coming into the room. Oh well, maybe Morgan could use her to test out whether or not her intuition was returning.

Under the cat's watchful eye, Morgan settled cross-legged into the middle of her bed. Her hand brushed the moonstone that was in her pocket. She'd worn all indigo. She was prepared for nurturing her gifts as she closed her eyes and slowed her breathing.

Hmm... now what to focus on? Oh, right, Belladonna. She would focus her mind on predicting what

Belladonna would do next. That sort of prediction was the part of her intuition that helped the most when confronting enemy paranormals: being able to sense their next move so they could take evasive measures.

Not that Belladonna was the enemy. Though from the cat's constant, annoying furtive glances, Morgan was starting to think of her as the enemy.

Breathe. Clear your mind. In. Out. Suddenly Morgan got a funny feeling deep in her chest. In her mind's eye, she saw an image of Belladonna sitting on one of the shelves on the left side of the built-in bookcases that flanked the fireplace.

"Meow."

Morgan's eyes flew open, searching the left side of the fireplace. Darn! No cat.

"MEOW!"

Her eyes tracked to the sound. Belladonna was lying on one of the shelves on the right side, her tail dangling over the edge, lazily swishing back and forth. Just like Morgan had seen in her mind's eye except on the wrong side. Did that mean her gifts were partially coming back?

Ding!

Morgan reached for her phone, her heart leaping when she saw it was a text from Alma.

I remembered something about the day Clementine died. Please come right away.

CHAPTER EIGHTEEN

*M*organ had raced out of the house using the excuse that she wanted to retrieve an herbal concoction that helped heighten her gifts at Sticks and Stones. The sisters were surprised, wondering why she'd never used that before. Morgan had lied once again, telling them it was something new that she was working on. Since they'd planned the confrontation for after the moon came up, she had about an hour.

She pulled into Alma's driveway with a heavy heart and the hope that tonight would be the last time she'd have to lie to her sisters. She didn't bother to hide her truck down the street. She didn't have time. And besides, so what if Alma recognized it now? She clearly had some evidence against Benedict.

Alma seemed nervous and grim. She let Morgan in and made sure to lock the doors behind her. Was she afraid Benedict might come along and discover she was giving Morgan evidence against him?

"You said you remembered something?" Morgan prompted as Alma led her back to the kitchen. Morgan didn't want to push. She knew how hard it was for people to admit that a loved one had committed an unspeakable act. The last thing she wanted was for Alma to clam up. Best to let her tell it in her own time.

Alma wrung her hands, the amethyst bracelet jangling. "Oh, it's all so awful." She glanced out the window toward Clementine's house.

Maybe if Morgan helped her along a bit. "Did you remember something about Benedict that afternoon at the bake sale? The afternoon Clementine was killed?"

Alma looked at her sharply. "Bennie? Why do you say that?"

Morgan pressed her lips together. Why was Alma acting like she didn't know a thing about Benedict? Denial? She thought Alma had summoned her to give her some evidence about him. Was she going to protect him with a lie? Morgan didn't have time for that. She might as well poke the hornet's nest now and help Alma come to her senses.

"Yes... well, I'd heard a rumor..." Morgan let her voice trail off to judge Alma's reaction.

Alma gave her a sharp look. Morgan could see the anguish in her eyes. "What do you mean?"

"That maybe Benedict had eyes for Clementine."

Alma scowled, but Morgan sensed a hesitation, as if Alma were warring with herself. Trying to come to terms with Benedict's betrayal. Wait. Could her intuition be returning? She'd sensed Alma's inner turmoil. That was a good thing, right? And perfect timing. Now all she had to do was let her intuition guide her as to how to get Alma to spit out her suspicions about Benedict.

"That's absurd. Benedict is my boyfriend." Alma said the words, but she didn't sound so sure of herself.

Morgan felt a stab of sympathy for the woman. Maybe she shouldn't have brought it up at all. But now that she had, it was best to plow on through to get the answers she needed. "So, you're sure there was nothing going on between Clementine and Benedict?"

"I told you no. Of course not. He was committed to me." Alma's eyes narrowed. "Where did you hear that anyway? Harriett? You'd do well to avoid the local gossip too. Harriett Fletcher likes to stick her nose where it doesn't belong. One of these days, she's going to poke it into the wrong place and have to pay the price."

For such a small, elderly woman, the vehemence on those words froze Morgan to the bone. Deep inside her, a wisp of power curled, a shadow of her normally strong intuition. The feeling of foreboding grew, as if it were trying desperately to tell her something. Alma now looked defensive and more than a tad angry as she fiddled with the amethyst bracelet at her wrist.

The bracelet. There was something about it. Her intuition was coming back. And then she felt the irresistible urge to look at the glass-door cabinets.

Everything on the shelves was perfectly placed. Even the canisters on the countertop were lined up perfectly and facing the same direction. The wisp inside her strengthened to a fog, filling every inch of Morgan's body, sending tingles of knowledge through her. Morgan would bet good money every item on those shelves and those canisters were equal distances apart too. Harriett had mentioned Alma's coffee cakes had all been perfectly wrapped and tied to match at the bake sale. Glancing around the kitchen, Morgan saw that not an item was out of place. It was obvious that Alma liked her things to be "just so." She herself had even said that she hated it when things were messy that day they'd run into her at Clementine's.

Morgan bit her lip to hold back the rush of adrenaline now pumping through her bloodstream. It was all starting to make sense.

"What is it, dear?" Alma asked, her tone neutral as she tracked Morgan's gaze to the cupboard. "You've gone awfully quiet all of a sudden. Something wrong?"

"No, nothing." Morgan stared at the bracelet. It was practically slipping off Alma's wrist. She knew why Alma had asked her to come, and it wasn't what she'd originally thought. Now she would have to be extremely clever and call upon her gifts—if they had in fact come back—to get evidence against Clementine's killer without ending up dead herself.

The image they'd seen in Rose's crystal ball flashed through her mind: Benedict walking in the snow near the big oak tree between Alma and Clementine's house. He'd been on Clementine's side, but not for the reason she'd suspected.

"I was just looking out the window over your sink. You've got a good view of Clementine's house through the tree line there, haven't you?"

"I suppose," Alma said, her frown deepening. "Why?"

"Sheriff White questioned me, that's all, after you reported seeing a truck similar to mine at Clementine's on the day of the murder. And you said you kept an eye on her place that day you stopped my sisters and me in the road too. I'm guessing that you probably saw all kinds of people going in and out of Clementine's house. Maybe even people you know. Maybe even Benedict."

"What?" Alma turned her bracelet around her wrist faster. "No. I don't think so. Why would he go over there? He didn't believe in all her mumbo-jumbo tricks. Besides, he was with me. We were a couple."

"Uh-huh." Morgan slipped her hand into her pocket to get strength from the moonstone. Her fingers brushed against the cold stone, and energy surged through her. She also felt around for her cell phone while she was at it. She might need that if she got in over her head.

"You'd originally told us that day in the street that you and Benedict were at the church bake sale at the time Clementine was killed, but when we spoke to Harriett Fletcher, she said she didn't see you or Benedict for a while after the argument. Could that argument have been about Clementine?"

"I told you that there was nothing between my Bennie and that woman." Alma pushed to her feet and stalked over to an ornately carved credenza and riffled through the drawer, the amethyst bracelet clanking against the edge.

"Oh no? Then what about that bracelet? Benedict didn't want us to mention it to you. At first, we thought it was because he was planning a surprise, but that wasn't it, was it? It was because the bracelet wasn't for you. It was for Clementine!" As soon as the words were out, Morgan was sure she was right. She knew exactly what had happened the day Clementine died. The mark on Clementine's wrist wasn't from a paranormal. It had happened when the killer had ripped the bracelet off. And that killer was Alma.

Alma spun around. Apparently she'd found what she had been looking for in the drawer, because she was pointing a dainty pearl-handled revolver in Morgan's direction.

Darn. Guess the old intuition wasn't working at full capacity, or she would have seen that one coming. Now what was she going to do?

* * *

MORGAN HELD her hands up in surrender until she could think of another way out of this.

"You Blackmoore girls really are too nosy for your own good," Alma snarled, moving closer. "Sheriff White is right to be wary of you and your family."

"*We've* done nothing wrong." Morgan closed her eyes and concentrated, calling on her gifts for all she was worth, hoping to strengthen the fog inside her into full power. If she could just figure out what move Alma would make beforehand, perhaps she could get the gun away from her.

The sinister snick of the hammer being cocked had her opening her eyes again. Morgan swallowed hard and fumbled for words. "You can't just shoot me. People will ask questions. My sisters will come looking for me."

"Then I guess I'll just have to tell them that Clementine's killer came back," Alma said, her tone growing more high-pitched and urgent. More desperate. "The killer's red Toyota is even parked in my driveway to prove it."

"What? You know darn well that truck was not there when Clementine was killed. You were supposed to be at the bake sale, so how could you have even seen it?" Morgan's eyes narrowed. "Of course, you were purposely vague about the timing of when you saw it, weren't you?"

Alma smiled, but it wasn't pretty. "Yes, I was. Though when I realized that my alibi was the bake sale, I had to act like a flustered old lady. I was actually hoping the sheriff would pin it on those hooligans that went over there that morning."

The paranormals? So, they really had gone to Clementine's.

At Morgan's quizzical look, Alma continued. "Yes, right after you left and before I saw Benedict go in, those nasty boys came over to Clementine's. I really did hear yelling then. They left in a hurry, and one of them lost his hat. I found it in the snow. Even planted it in her kitchen. Cops must not be too smart though, as it doesn't appear as if they ever followed up."

Too busy trying to pin it on me, Morgan thought.

"But I guess that doesn't matter now." Alma waved the gun maniacally. "You've given me the perfect opportunity to stop you from snooping and present the cops with their killer. I'll tell them that the murderer must've spotted me that day and needed to finish the job. I killed them in self-defense. Sheriff White will believe me. She can't stand you or your family anyway, and besides, you've been accused of murder before. Now get up and move."

Alma gestured toward the back door with the gun, and Morgan rose and headed that way, her mind reeling.

"I'll tell the sheriff you were trying to break in," Alma said, moving in closer to Morgan now. "I'll say I recognized your truck from the day of the murder and was frightened. You came at me, trying to attack me, and I had no choice."

As the seconds ticked by, Morgan tried harder and harder to summon her gifts, to focus on the gun, to try and get the weapon away from Alma. Rose's words from the other night echoed in her head.

Focus on the victories.

Her tea had worked on Jolene. Her gut had told her to look at the cups in the cabinet. She'd felt there was something about the bracelet.

Her gifts were still there. She just had to believe in them.

First, though, she needed to keep Alma busy talking so she wouldn't shoot.

"If you're going to kill me anyway, why not tell me what really happened? Get your story out," Morgan urged, stalling for time. "Holding all those messy secrets inside must feel terrible for someone who loves order as much as you do."

Alma gave her a steely stare, her jaw tight. For a moment, Morgan thought she might just pull the trigger. Time seemed to slow, and Morgan braced herself for the pain.

But then the older woman huffed, and truth flowed out.

"Like I said to the sheriff, I saw your truck there. I like to keep track of who's coming and going from Clementine's because there's so much customer traffic, and it has become a hobby of mine to call the cops and complain about it. Plus, I'd just had my weekly reading at Rose Degarmo's, and she'd mentioned my love life might be rocky. Of course, I'd heard the rumors spreading about my Bennie and Clementine, and I wanted to make sure for myself they weren't true." Alma's lips compressed into a thin white line before a small hiccupping sob escaped her. If the woman hadn't been pointing a loaded gun at Morgan's chest, she almost might have felt sorry for her. Almost. "After you left, those hooligans showed up at Clementine's, but they didn't stay long. Then Benedict drove up the street. We were supposed to go to the bake sale together, and I thought he came early because he couldn't wait to see me, but he didn't park where he usually did. He turned off on a side street. Looking back now, I know that's because he didn't want me to see his car." Her tone deepened, became more brittle. "He walked through the woods and went into Clementine's house through the back door."

Morgan's gaze flicked from Alma's face to the gun still pointed at her chest.

"Naturally, I was upset. Benedict was *my* boyfriend. I loved him first. Then at the bake sale, when I questioned him about it, he lied." Alma's expression hardened. "That's when I knew there really was something going on."

"So you snuck away from the bake sale and killed her?"

"After we fought, Bennie stormed off. I was mad, so I went over to confront Clementine. She tried to hide it, play it off, said she'd turned him down, didn't like him like that. Had never liked him like that. She even made tea like we were old friends or something. I wasn't having it." Tears streamed down Alma's face now, and her gaze grew distant as she remembered her crimes. "We argued. Clementine told me all that, but I knew then that my Bennie liked her better. Our fight got nastier, and that's when the truth came out. She said Bennie was afraid of me. Said he told her he was going to break things off with me but was scared of my vindictive nature." She snorted. "He was right. I am vindictive. He should've been scared. They both should've been scared. Clementine lied, telling me she had no interest in Benedict, but I knew the truth. I knew why Rose hesitated at my reading when she looked at my love line. I knew it was about my relationship with Bennie."

"How did you kill her?" Morgan asked not because she wanted the gory details but to keep her assailant busy. The tingles of power flowing through her were stronger now, strengthening, reemerging, but she needed more time. "And how did a piece of one of Rose's tarot cards get there?"

Alma laughed, a maniacal, unpleasant sound. "I showed it to her. I'd swiped it from my reading earlier with Rose. The ten of swords. A sure sign of betrayal, of being stabbed in the back by those you trusted. Clementine didn't buy it, of course. She'd never liked Rose Degarmo, never believed in her gifts. She laughed at me. She took the tarot card and ripped it up. Tossed it in the air like confetti."

"So Clementine was acting like she wasn't interested in Bennie so that the rumor mill would think nothing was going on? Buying time until he could break it off with you?" Morgan asked.

"Yep. But I guess she didn't want to pretend anymore. That's when she flaunted the amethyst bracelet in my face. Bennie had given it to her. That bracelet *should* have been for me. And that's when I saw red."

The older lady shifted slightly, still keeping the gun trained on Morgan. "I'd had it with her and her snide remarks and her lies. I grabbed a heavy iron pot from her stove and clonked Clementine over the head with it when she was busy admiring her bracelet. At first, I'd not meant to kill her, just hurt her like she'd hurt me, but then she didn't move, didn't breathe. Good riddance, I say. I picked up all the pieces of the tarot card, washed out the teacups to remove any of my DNA. I don't watch all those cop shows on TV for nothing. Then I put them back in her cupboard and left the way I'd come, but not before ripping the bracelet off her wrist." Alma glanced down at the bracelet. "It should have been mine anyway."

Alma was herding her toward the back door, and Morgan made one last-ditch attempt to distract Alma by playing on her jealousy. "My sister told me that Benedict had that bracelet especially made for Clementine. And a matching pair of earrings. He must've cared for her deeply."

Alma's hand flew to her ears. No earrings there. She grimaced and waved the gun at Morgan. "Open the back door. Time to get this done."

Oops. Maybe she shouldn't have said something that would make Alma so angry. Morgan opened the door as told, feeling suddenly calm, as if her intuition was telling her it would be all right.

Frigid air blasted into the room as Morgan stepped out onto the back stoop, beyond grateful she'd not taken her coat off inside. Alma was behind her and had to be freezing in just that sweater, but she gave no indication of being aware of the cold temperature. Murdering someone probably did that to a person, Morgan supposed.

"Out!" Alma shoved Morgan hard from behind, but the move caused Alma to slip on the icy stoop. Morgan seized her opportunity and whirled fast, lunging for the gun. Alma regained her footing and moved back, but Morgan's gifts came through at last. A premonition flashed through her mind like lightning: Alma pointing the gun at Morgan's head.

Using that information, Morgan ducked low and rushed the older woman, tackling her to the ground. The gun flew from Alma's hand, and they grappled for it in the snow. More premonitions flooded Morgan's mind, like a bottle of champagne that was shaken to the point of bursting. All of Alma's future moves cascaded over Morgan like a tsunami, allowing her to wrestle the gun away and restrain Alma with an old garden hose lying in the back yard.

Out of breath yet exhilarated at the same time, Morgan stood beside a tied-up and struggling Alma on the frozen ground and pulled out her cell phone to dial 9-1-1. "Yes, I'd like to report the capture of Clementine Vega's murderer, please."

CHAPTER NINETEEN

The next day, Morgan and her sisters were sitting at the house under their blankets before another roaring fire with fresh hot cocoa in their mugs while fluffy white flakes of snow swirled outside the window.

Belladonna was once again curled up at Morgan's feet, but her usual accusing glare was gone, and she purred happily. It was as if the cat knew that her gifts were back and everything would be okay now. Or at least that she wasn't outwardly lying to her sisters anymore.

"So, explain to me how you figured out Alma was the killer," Jolene said.

Morgan went over how she'd put the clues together from what Harriett had told them and from what they'd seen at Rose's in the crystal ball. About how, at the crucial moment, her intuition kicked into hyperdrive, and everything just fell into place. It wasn't the whole truth—hopefully that would never come out—but it was enough to satisfy their curiosity.

"And you just figured all this out when you went back to Sticks and Stones to get that intuition-boosting herbal concoction?" Jolene asked.

"Yep." Morgan nodded, her gut tightening at the lie. Hopefully this would be the last one. "I took some of it and then... bam! It all kicked in. Well, except I thought it was Benedict and not Alma. Guess I still have some work to do nurturing my gifts." At least that was one part she didn't need to lie about.

"Don't we all?" Johanna shot Morgan a knowing look as she slid a plate of sugar cookies onto the coffee table before returning to the kitchen. Did her mother suspect what had been going on with her? She couldn't tell, and if her intuition knew, it wasn't signaling.

"That was pretty dangerous going there alone, sis. Even if you thought Benedict was the killer. Who's to say that Alma might not have tried to act in her man's best interest to protect him?" Fiona asked, giving her a disapproving look. "You should've called one of us. We would've had your back."

"I know." Morgan reached over to snag a cookie. "I just wanted to go by her place on the way home before we got into it with those paranormals. Just to ask a few questions about Benedict, because I figured if I was right, then we didn't need to stir up trouble with the treasure seekers. By the time I realized the killer was really Alma, it was too late. I was already in her house, and she was right there. It wasn't like I could just pull out my phone casually to call for help. Plus, it was my vehicle Alma said she saw that day, and that's what got us all involved in this in the first place. I felt like it was my responsibility to get us out of it."

"But you weren't there that day," Celeste said, watching her closely. "Right?"

"Right. I guess there really is another Toyota similar to mine." The lie was bitter on her tongue, and more guilt soon followed, but if she opened that can of worms, she'd have to come clean about all of it, and she didn't want to go there. Not now when she finally had her powers back. Or so it seemed. She wasn't exactly sure she could trust them to be back for good. Just to be on the safe side about that, she'd done another little experiment to be sure things were back to normal, in the form of a special herb added to the hot cocoa her sisters were drinking at the moment.

Belladonna turned to her with an admonishing glare. Oops.

Liar!

Morgan frowned. Yeah, that almost sounded like she was hearing the cat's thoughts.

She narrowed her gaze on the feline and concentrated,

but nothing else came. Probably just her guilty conscience. But maybe she should file that away for future reference.

Even though her gifts had returned, she planned to stick with Rose's advice to avoid the same problems in the future. And if new gifts were also emerging—like animal telepathy, perhaps—she wanted to be prepared.

She tuned back into the conversation around her and found her sisters were still rehashing all the clues they'd had in the case.

Fiona chuckled and winked at Morgan. "Bet Sheriff White wasn't too happy about finding out she'd been pursuing the wrong suspect all this time."

"Nope." Morgan grinned. "Not much she can do, though, since Alma made a full confession. We'll have to watch our backs in the future though. She's turning out to be every bit as bad as Overton."

"I heard through the grapevine at the yoga studio that poor Benedict is quite upset," Celeste said. "Harriett said it turned out he really did love Clementine and didn't know what to do when she was killed. He never dreamed it was Alma who murdered her."

"I still wonder about those two paranormal energies I sensed at Clementine's that day though," Jolene said. "And the energy down at the beach. I mean, I guess they aren't involved in what happened to poor Clementine, but still. It's weird."

Biting her lip, Morgan stared down into her cocoa. She'd been worried Mateo might've confessed to Jolene about them going to Clementine's house that day, but apparently, he hadn't. Good. They'd keep each other's secrets. For now, anyway. She focused on the beach energy instead to distract her sister. "I agree. That whole thing with the dig site by the shore is strange. We should keep an eye on that."

"Definitely," Jolene agreed. "That treasure might be more important than we think if there's a relic included in the treasure."

Several times in the past year, the sisters had been called upon by the government agency that Luke worked for to retrieve certain paranormally infused relics that were important to world peace. Or at least the government's version of it. If Jolene's speculation was correct, their next assignment might be very close to home. And that was fine with Morgan, especially now that her gifts were back, and there was no way she was going to let them slip away again.

"Excuse me a minute," Fiona said, tossing aside her blanket. "Potty break."

"Oh, me too," Celeste said, following close on her heels. "You take the powder room down here. I'll use the one upstairs."

"And that leaves me with the bathroom over by the

library." Jolene set her cocoa aside and stood. "You need to go too, sis?"

"No. You guys go on ahead. I'm good." Morgan waited until her youngest sister had left the room before breaking into a full grin. Looked like the herbal concoction she'd slipped into the cocoa had worked. She had her gifts back.

"Meow."

She looked down to see Belladonna frowning up at her, recrimination radiating from her ice-blue eyes. Morgan scooped the cat up and put her in her lap, stroking her soft fur. Morgan leaned down and whispered in her ear. "You be quiet. You can keep a secret for me, can't you?"

Belladonna stared at her for a few seconds, then Morgan swore the cat nodded ever so slightly before turning in a circle and curling up in her lap.

Morgan smiled as she relaxed back in the chair, soothed by the cat's purring vibrations. Yep, things were good again. Belladonna was on her side. Mateo had kept their pact. Her gifts were back. And her sisters never had to know she'd almost lost them.

****

the lowest possible price, plus as a benefit for signing up today, I will send you a copy of a new Leighann Dobbs book that hasn't been published anywhere...yet!
http://www.leighanndobbs.com/newsletter

Join my readers group on Facebook and get the inside scoop on my books -
https://www.facebook.com/groups/ldobbsreaders

If you want to receive a text message on your cell phone when I have a new release, text COZYMYSTERY to 88202 (sorry, this only works for US cell phones!)

Want more Blackmoore Sister's adventures? Buy the rest of the books in the series:

Dead Wrong
Dead & Buried
Dead Tide
Buried Secrets
Deadly Intentions
A Grave Mistake
Spell Found
Fatal Fortune

ALSO BY LEIGHANN DOBBS

Cozy Mysteries

Mystic Notch

Cat Cozy Mystery Series

* * *

Ghostly Paws

A Spirited Tail

A Mew To A Kill

Paws and Effect

Probable Paws

Whisker of a Doubt

Silver Hollow

Paranormal Cozy Mystery Series

***

A Spell of Trouble (Book 1)

Spell Disaster (Book 2)

Nothing to Croak About (Book 3)

Cry Wolf (Book 4)

Shear Magic (Book 5)

Kate Diamond Mystery Adventures

***

Hidden Agemda (Book 1)

Ancient Hiss Story (Book 2)

Heist Society (Book 3)

Mooseamuck Island Cozy Mystery Series

* * *

A Zen For Murder

A Crabby Killer

A Treacherous Treasure

Blackmoore Sisters
Cozy Mystery Series

* * *

Dead Wrong

Dead & Buried

Dead Tide

Buried Secrets

Deadly Intentions

A Grave Mistake

Spell Found

Fatal Fortune

Lexy Baker Cozy Mystery Series

* * *

Lexy Baker Cozy Mystery Series Boxed Set Vol 1 (Books 1-4)

Or buy the books separately:

Killer Cupcakes

Dying For Danish

Murder, Money and Marzipan

3 Bodies and a Biscotti

Brownies, Bodies & Bad Guys

Bake, Battle & Roll

Wedded Blintz

Scones, Skulls & Scams

Ice Cream Murder

Mummified Meringues

Brutal Brulee (Novella)

No Scone Unturned

Cream Puff Killer

Hazel Martin Historical Mystery Series

***

Murder at Lowry House (book 1)

Murder by Misunderstanding (book 2)

Lady Katherine Regency Mysteries

***

An Invitation to Murder (Book 1)

The Baffling Burglaries of Bath (Book 2)

Murder at the Ice Ball (Book 3)

Sam Mason Mysteries

(As L. A. Dobbs)

***

Telling Lies (Book 1)

Keeping Secrets (Book 2)

Exposing Truths (Book 3)

Betraying Trust (Book 4)

Killing Dreams (Book 5)

Magical Romance with a Touch of Mystery

✿✿✿

Something Magical

Curiously Enchanted

Romantic Comedy

✿✿✿

Corporate Chaos Series

In Over Her Head (book 1)

Can't Stand the Heat (book 2)

What Goes Around Comes Around (book 3)

Careful What You Wish For (4)

Contemporary Romance

✿✿✿

Reluctant Romance

Sweet Romance (Written As Annie Dobbs)

Firefly Inn Series

***

Another Chance (Book 1)

Another Wish (Book 2)

Hometown Hearts Series

***

No Getting Over You (Book 1)

A Change of Heart (Book 2)

***

Sweetrock Sweet and Spicy Cowboy Romance

Some Like It Hot

Too Close For Comfort

────

Regency Romance

* * *

Scandals and Spies Series:

Kissing The Enemy

Deceiving the Duke

Tempting the Rival

Charming the Spy

Pursuing the Traitor

Captivating the Captain

The Unexpected Series:

An Unexpected Proposal

An Unexpected Passion

Dobbs Fancytales:

Dobbs Fancytales Boxed Set Collection

———

Western Historical Romance

❋❋❋

Goldwater Creek Mail Order Brides:

Faith

American Mail Order Brides Series:

Chevonne: Bride of Oklahoma

———————

Magical Romance with a Touch of Mystery

A NOTE FROM THE AUTHOR

I hope you enjoyed reading this book as much as I enjoyed writing it. This is the eighth book in the Blackmoore sisters mystery series and I have a whole bunch more planned!

The setting for this book series is based on one of my favorite places in the world - Ogunquit Maine. Of course, I changed some of the geography around to suit my story, and changed the name of the town to Noquitt but the basics are there. Anyone familiar with Ogunquit will recognize some of the landmarks I have in the book.

The house the sisters live in sits at the very end of Perkins Cove and I was always fascinated with it as a kid. Of course, back then it was a mysterious, creepy old house that was privately owned and I was dying to go in there. I'm sure it must have had an attic stuffed full of antiques just like in the book!

Today, it's been all modernized and updated—I think you can even rent it out for a summer vacation. In the book the house looks different and it's also set high up on a cliff (you'll see why in a later book) where in real life it's not. I've also made the house much older to suit my story.

Also, if you like this book, you might like my Mystic Notch series which is set in the White Mountains of New Hampshire and filled with magic and cats. You can find out more about this series on my website.

This book has been through many edits with several people and even some software programs, but since nothing is infallible (even the software programs) you might catch a spelling error or mistake and, if you do, I sure would appreciate it if you let me know - you can contact me at lee@leighanndobbs.com.

Oh, and I love to connect with my readers so please do visit me on facebook at http://www.facebook.com/leighanndobbsbooks or at my website http://www.leighanndobbs.com.

Want a free never-before-published novella from my Lexy Baker culinary mystery series? Go to: http://www.leighanndobbs.com/newsletter and enter your email address to signup - I promise never to share it and I only send emails every couple of weeks so I won't fill up your inbox.

ABOUT THE AUTHOR

Leighann Dobbs discovered her passion for writing after a twenty year career as a software engineer. She lives in New Hampshire with her husband Bruce, their trusty Chihuahua mix Mojo and beautiful rescue cat, Kitty. When she's not reading, gardening or selling antiques, she likes to write cozy mysteries and romances. Find out about her latest books and how to get discounts on them by signing up at:

http://www.leighanndobbs.com/newsletter

Connect with Leighann on Facebook:

http://facebook.com/leighanndobbsbooks

Join her private readers group on Facebook:

https://www.facebook.com/groups/ldobbsreaders/

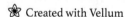